THEIRS TO TAKE
FIRST EDITION September 2017
THEIRS TO TAKE © Laura Kaye.
ALL RIGHTS RESERVED.

No part or whole of this book may be used, reproduced, distributed, or transmitted in any manner whatsoever without written permission of the author except in the case of brief quotations embodied in critical articles or reviews. The unauthorized reproduction or distribution of this copyrighted work via electronic or mechanical means is a violation of international copyright law and subjects the violator to severe fines and/or imprisonment. If you are reading the ebook, it is licensed for your personal enjoyment only. The ebook may not be re-sold or given away to other people. If you would like to share the ebook, please purchase an additional copy for each person you share it with. Please do not participate in piracy of copyrighted materials in violation of the author's rights. Thank you for respecting the author's work.

The characters and events portrayed in this book are fictional and/or are used fictitiously and are solely the product of the author's imagination. Any similarity to persons living or dead, places, businesses, events, or locales is purely coincidental.

Cover Design and Interior Format

To Colleen —

THEIRS TO Take

xo, Laura Kaye

NEW YORK TIMES BESTSELLING AUTHOR
LAURA KAYE

Praise for the Blasphemy Series

"Laura Kaye shows her mastery of the BDSM world. I'm eagerly anticipating more in this bold new series!"

~ Cherise Sinclair, *NYT* Bestselling Author of
the MASTERS OF THE SHADOWLANDS SERIES

"Smoldering and sexy, Laura Kaye's Blasphemy series is everything I look for in a romance. Haunted heroes and strong heroines populate this one of a kind club and I can't wait to see the big bad Doms fall one by one."

~ Lexi Blake, *NYT* Bestselling Author of the
MASTERS AND MERCENARIES SERIES

Hot Contemporary Romance
by
Laura Kaye

Blasphemy Series
HARD TO SERVE – A HARD INK CROSSOVER
BOUND TO SUBMIT
MASTERING HER SENSES
EYES ON YOU

Raven Riders Series
HARD AS STEEL – A HARD INK CROSSOVER
RIDE HARD
RIDE ROUGH
RIDE WILD

Hard Ink Series
HARD AS IT GETS
HARD AS YOU CAN
HARD TO HOLD ON TO
HARD TO COME BY
HARD TO BE GOOD
HARD TO LET GO
HARD AS STEEL – A RAVEN RIDERS CROSSOVER
HARD EVER AFTER
HARD TO SERVE – A BLASPHEMY CROSSOVER

Hearts in Darkness Duet
HEARTS IN DARKNESS
LOVE IN THE LIGHT

Heroes Series
HER FORBIDDEN HERO
ONE NIGHT WITH A HERO

Stand Alone Titles
DARE TO RESIST
JUST GOTTA SAY

Dedication

To love. Is love is love is love is love.

Chapter 1

HARTLEY FARREN STARED AT THE wreck of her catamaran and tried not to cry. Or scream. Or punch something with her bare fist.

She'd done everything right to prepare for the hurricane that had come through two days before. Baltimore's Lighthouse Point's marina provided an excellent safe harbor with a fantastic track record of low storm damage, and she'd been sure to use long dock lines to allow the boat to rise and fall during the storm surge. But none of that mattered when someone *else* wasn't as diligent in their preparations. And the consequence had been that another boat had lost its mooring and the wind had driven it into her *Far 'n Away*, damaging the port side.

"I'm really sorry," the other owner said for the dozenth time. "I told Charlie we needed more lines, but he said the Chesapeake never gets hit that badly." In her sixties and sweet as pie, the lady made it hard for Hartley to stay mad when she revealed that their own boat, a total loss, had been their only residence for the past eighteen months, leaving them essentially homeless. They stood and watched while the lady's husband worked with the harbor master to have the wreck towed away.

"I know," Hartley said. "It'll all work out somehow. For both of us."

Hartley had to believe that. Because that cat was her whole life.

Her father had left his charter business to her when he died three years before. Now, that business and that boat provided her whole income and allowed her to keep her grandmother, who suffered from Alzheimer's, in a lovely assisted-living community.

But now Hartley was dead in the water. Or, at least, her charter business was. Until she dealt with the insurance claims and found someone to do the repairs. Both were sure to be a pain in the butt following a big storm.

Hartley sighed. Neither crying, screaming, nor punching something was going to make anything better. And she'd certainly fared better than some others—she had to be grateful for that. She slid the business card detailing the couple's contact information into her pocket and said her good-byes, and then she made her way to the marina office.

"Hi Linda," she said to the office manager she'd met for the first time when she was only eight or nine. Back then, Hartley had been her dad's "first mate" as much as going to school and playing field hockey had allowed.

"How bad is it, hon?" Linda tucked the gray hair of her bob behind her ears as she came around her desk. The office was a big square with four desks, the back two partially hidden behind cubicle partitions. Normally, the room was bright and airy, as windows lined the two exterior walls, but boards currently covered the glass, making it feel like nighttime in the middle of the day.

"Fixable. That's not the problem, though. The problem is whether it can be fixed fast. There's no avoiding having to cancel several weeks of charters, but I'll be sunk if I have to pull out of the sailboat show and the Sailing University courses I'm teaching." Thank God she'd been smart enough to buy business interruption insurance, but that was only going to cover her so far. If she didn't get the *Far 'n Away* repaired within three weeks, well, she wasn't going to think about that. Not yet.

"What can I do to help?" Linda asked, giving her the same affectionate, grandmotherly look she'd been giving her for the past twenty-plus years. It was an affection born not only from their long-time friendship, but from the fact that Linda and her father had been close—close enough that Hartley suspected something romantic between them before her dad unexpectedly died of a heart attack. Since then, Linda had been one of the few people who seemed to understand the grief and loneliness Hartley had been working through.

"Can I borrow a desk and your Wi-Fi?" Hartley gestured to the messenger bag on her shoulder. "I have my laptop and I'd love to dive into finding a place that can do the work."

"That's easy. Of course. You know your way around. Make yourself at home."

"Thanks, Linda. What would I do without you?" she asked as she sat at the more private desk behind Linda's.

The older lady peered around the corner at her and smirked. "Says the woman who spends days and days alone at sea. You'd get by just fine. You don't *need* me, Hartley. I'm just your cheerleading section."

Hartley chuckled. "Well, I appreciate that, too." She set up and turned on her laptop. She'd just looked up the contact information for her insurance company when Linda placed a steaming mug on the desk.

"I'm also your deliverer of mint tea." Linda winked.

"And clearly also a goddess," Hartley said, taking the cup in hand. She adored the feeling of warm ceramic against her palms. "Can't forget that one."

"Naturally," Linda said. "Hey, since you're here, can you let anyone who comes in know I'll be right back? I have to run over to the Harbor Master's office for a short meeting."

"You got it," Hartley said, sipping at the sweet, minty tea. A moment later, the front door opened and closed, leaving Hartley alone to figure out who was going to be her savior.

Scheduling a time to meet with the insurance adjuster turned out to be easy enough. But, thirty minutes later, she'd called a dozen boat repair shops and only found two willing to consider the work—but neither could even come look at the cat for almost a week, nor commit to completing the repairs within the next three.

Hartley dropped her head into her hands and heaved a deep breath. In the quiet, the soft opening and closing of the outer door reached her ears. "Hey, Linda," she called. Then, to herself, "What am I going to do?"

"Hey, are you okay?"

The voice was deep, male, and definitely not Linda's. Hartley's gaze whipped up. And up. To find a tall and incredibly sexy man standing in the doorway to her cubicle. Sun-kissed shoulder-length blond hair framed a ruggedly masculine face and intense gray eyes that were at once inquisitive and observing. Broad shoulders and defined muscles pulled taut a heather-gray T-shirt with a single word across the chest: *NAVY*. His forearms and legs beneath khaki cargo shorts were toned and tanned, as if he spent a lot of time in the sun.

"Uh, hi. Yes. Sorry. I'm kinda in my own world here. Did you need Linda?" Hartley managed as she pushed to her feet. At five-five, she wasn't short, but his impressive height made her tilt her head back to meet his assessing gaze.

He shook his head. "I was coming by to see if she needed a hand with anything around the marina."

"Oh. Wow. I'm sure she'd appreciate that. She stepped out to a meeting but she should be back soon if you'd like to wait." Despite his selfless reason for being there, the man made Hartley nervous. She wasn't sure why. Maybe it was the intensity behind those odd, gray eyes. Or the way he towered over her. Or how freaking good-looking he was.

"I'll do that. Thanks."

"Sure," she said. But he didn't leave. "Um, anything else I can do for you?"

His gaze stayed glued to hers, but she had the oddest feeling that he was checking her out nonetheless. He smiled and shook his head. And, *man*, was his smile a stunner, highlighting the strong angles of his jaw and charming her with the way the right side of his mouth lifted higher than the left. He thumbed over his shoulder. "I'll just grab a seat."

And then he disappeared from her little doorway.

Hartley was half tempted to peer around the corner and watch him walk away. Just to see if the rear view was as impressive as the front.

On a sigh, she dropped back into her chair. And even though her thoughts should've returned to the huge problem of fixing her boat, they lingered on the Good Samaritan currently making small noises on the other side of the room. Who was he? Hartley had essentially grown up around this marina. Even though she couldn't say she knew everyone here, she still recognized most of the regulars. And she'd never seen Mr. Tall, Blond, and Ruggedly Handsome before.

Her cell phone buzzed, pulling her from her thoughts.

"Hello?" she answered.

"Mrs. Farren, this is Ed Stark returning your call from Stark Restoration."

Hope rushed through Hartley. "Hi, Mr. Stark. Thanks for calling back so quickly. And, please, call me Hartley." Being called 'missus' was almost laughable when she couldn't remember the last time she'd gone on a date. With rebuilding the business after her father's death and taking care of her grandmother, Hartley didn't have time to date. Or, at least, she hadn't made the time. Not that she'd had any prospects motivating her to do so. Shaking the thoughts away, she filled the man in on the damage and the challenge of her timeline.

"I might be able to get someone out to take a look at your boat by the end of the week, but you're at least the tenth call I've had today. I wouldn't be able to guarantee a completion date without assessing the damage, and I've got a number of other repair jobs ahead of yours."

It was the same thing all the others had told her. And Hartley got it. She did. It wasn't anyone else's problem that she depended on the *Far 'n Away* for her livelihood. Or that she'd put most of what her father left her three years ago into her grandmother's nursing home and a bigger boat that could carry more passengers. Or that July had been so rainy that her normal charter business had been halved. Or that she needed the extra income that the sailboat show and Sailing University courses would bring in to make it through the leaner winter months.

Just then, the front door opened again. "Hartley, I'm back. Sorry I was gone so long." This time, it was definitely Linda. "Oh, Jonathan. How are you? How did you guys make out in the storm?"

"Our shop's fine, ma'am," the man said. "Thanks for asking." Jonathan. Jonathan who apparently had a shop somewhere in the marina?

Even more curious about him, Hartley stepped out of her cubicle and tried not to stare. Or drool. She forced her gaze to her friend. "Hey, Linda. Everything go okay?"

"Oh, yes. Just little fires everywhere that need put out," Linda said, dropping a legal pad full of notes onto her desk. "Were you able to find anyone to do the work?"

Hartley's shoulders fell. "No. No one can even look before Friday." And with a hole in the side of the cat, who knew how much more damage it might sustain over those four days.

Linda frowned, and then her gaze swung to Jonathan. "Have you two met yet?"

That intense gray-eyed gaze landed on Hartley, unleashing a

whirl of butterflies in her belly. "Haven't had the pleasure to do so officially," Jonathan said.

It was a simple statement. But something about the word *pleasure* from that man's mouth made a tingle run down her spine. It'd clearly been too long since she'd been on a date. Or been kissed. And waaaay too long since she'd last had sex. Embarrassingly long. Like, she didn't even want to admit to herself how long.

(Fifteen months. Oy.)

With that fantastic thought in mind, all Hartley managed to say was, "Uh, hi. Again." *Wow, that was some brilliant conversation right there, Hartley.* She chuckled to cover how much she wanted to duck back into the cubicle and bang her head against the desk.

He grinned. "Hi. Again. I'm Jonathan Allen."

"Hartley Farren." Feeling Linda's amused gaze on her, she cleared her throat. "You have a shop in the marine center?"

He nodded. "A&R Builds and Restoration."

"Jonathan and his partner Cruz own the business that moved into the old Stanton space at the beginning of the summer," Linda added helpfully.

Hartley's eyes went wide as her heart kicked into a sprint. "*You* do builds and restoration?"

He chuckled. "As the name suggests."

She didn't mind the teasing, not when he might be able to help her. "Then you might be my new favorite person."

"Is that right?"

The office phone rang, and Linda excused herself to answer it.

Hartley stepped closer to Jonathan. Why did that make her feel like she was approaching a usually friendly but sometimes lethal animal? Her stomach did a little flip. "Yes, because I need a huge, huge, *gigantic* favor."

He arched a sexy brow. "And if I do this favor, will I *officially* be your favorite person?"

She grinned, enjoying his playfulness—and the fact that he was entertaining doing her a favor when they barely knew each other. "Without question. I'll even make you a certificate. *Jonathan Allen. Hartley Farren's Favorite Person.*"

That crooked smile emerged again, and hope flooded through her. "Hmm. I don't know. I mean, a certificate is nice and all, but..."

Hartley braced her hands on her hips. "Are you teasing me? Because that would be evil, Jonathan, and you don't strike me as an evil man." Now *she* arched a brow.

His chuckle this time was different. Deeper. Grittier. Sexier. With an undercurrent of...something she didn't understand. "You never know, Hartley."

Her stomach did a little flip, because it had been eons since anyone had flirted with her. Or, at least, since she'd allowed herself to notice. Let alone a man this attractive. "Oh, come on. Can I at least tell you what my favor is?" she asked.

Those gray eyes sparkled with amusement. "Well, I couldn't help but overhear your phone conversation, so I have an inkling."

Wait. He *knew* what she needed and still hadn't said no? Hope and anticipation rushed through her, making her feel restless and brave. "Then if my awesome certificate idea isn't enough, what can I offer to convince you to walk out to my slip and take a look at my catamaran?"

That eyebrow arched again, and Hartley suddenly felt like they'd been playing chess—and her words had just allowed him to put her in checkmate. But still, he didn't make any claims of her.

She stepped closer and dared to flirt back. "Jonathan. Mr. Allen. *Mr. Allen, My Already Officially Favorite Person*, are you going to make me beg? Because that wouldn't be very nice," she added playfully.

Those gray eyes flared. She would've sworn they did. He bit back a chuckle as he shook his head. And when his words came, they were filled with a deep intensity that made her shiver. "Why don't you show me your boat, Hartley, and then I'll answer your questions."

Chapter 2

JONATHAN STARED AT THE PLASTIC-COVERED hole in the side of the catamaran. Luckily, the impact had been above the water line, but as he surveyed the less-catastrophic damage surrounding the hole, he felt the owner's pain. He certainly felt the owner's eyes. On him.

And he was intrigued.

"Boat's a beauty," he said, his gaze swinging from the Lipari's white hull, with its colorful scrollwork around the logo, to Hartley. Who was also a beauty. Long-wavy brown hair, tied up in a ponytail. Big, expressive brown eyes and lashes for days. A perfect bow-shaped mouth, and a habit of biting the side of her bottom lip when she was deep in thought. She was casual in jean shorts that revealed toned, tanned legs, an oversized sweatshirt with the neck cut wide, exposing the colorful blue-and-purple edge of a tattoo on her shoulder, and a pair of well-worn boat shoes.

Every bit as appealing, as she spoke about the thirty-nine-foot multi-hull, was her obvious love for the sea and sailing. Loves that Jonathan shared. Loves that, along with love of country, had led him to college at the Naval Academy and eight years of active-duty service before he and his best friend got out and went into business for themselves.

"I bought her three years ago. Used a lot of my savings," Hartley said. "But she was worth it." She sighed. "Let me show you what I'm dealing with on the inside. She took on some water."

He nodded, his gut souring for her. Brackish water damage sometimes made it smarter to write a boat off as a constructive total loss. "Lead the way."

She moved around the vessel with utter competence and confidence, obviously at home on the deck of a boat. "I cleaned up as much as I could, but it was wet inside for probably thirty-six hours before I could get to it."

They descended the companionway into the salon, richly appointed with honey-colored wood, black countertops and cushions on the L-shaped corner bench seat around the table. Surrounding windows no doubt offered fantastic views when underway. Hartley led him down a shorter companionway on the port side and moved fore, past a built-in desk and cabinetry to a double cabin, where unnatural, muted light shone through the plastic.

They squeezed together into the narrow space before the wooden platform bed, already warping from hours of holding water.

Hartley sighed. "So…yeah."

"Yeah," he said, his mind already working over all that would be required to make the *Far 'n Away* seaworthy again. For starters, this whole assembly was going to have to be removed and replaced to ensure hidden mold didn't grow. Given the quality of the wood, and the details of the build—like the built-in chest of drawers at the foot of the bed and the way the molding had been designed as one continuous piece that extended into the adjacent hallway—it wasn't a small job.

"I know it's a lot," she said, echoing his thoughts.

It was. And since they'd just taken on a new custom-build

client with a January delivery, Jonathan shouldn't even be considering taking this on, too. But, damnit, he wanted to help Hartley. They were both part of this community here at the marine center, and it was a neighborly thing to do. And, of course, he knew she was out of options given her time constraints.

But those weren't the only reasons. If he was being honest with himself, he liked her. He was attracted to her. Both of which tempted him to want to get to know her better. Even if that probably wasn't smart, not when his tastes ran in directions that the average woman didn't share—and just because they shared an obvious interest in sailing, he had absolutely no reason to assume that he might have those *other* interests in common with Hartley Farren, too.

Damnit. He still wanted to do this for her. But not without consulting Cruz. "My partner needs to see this before I can make a decision," he said, looking at her. "He and I do everything together."

Expression earnest, she nodded. "Of course. I understand."

Oh, how he doubted that. "Let me see if he's still over at the shop." Jonathan put his cell to his ear and prepared to get his ass handed to him for considering this.

"Hey, man, what's up?" Cruz answered, a slight accent to his words.

"You have time to come over to the Lighthouse slips?" Jonathan mentally cringed as he waited for Cruz's obvious question.

"Why? What's up?" he asked.

"I need you to take a look at a boat."

A beat passed, and then an exasperated chuckle. "What are you getting sucked into over there, my man?"

He'd find out soon enough, and no doubt it'd come with a shit-ton of ribbing. "Just come. East Marina, pier K, slip 55."

"Okay, but tell me this, what's her name?" And there it was, already starting.

Jonathan glanced at Hartley, who stood with her arms crossed, trying but failing to act nonchalant, like she wasn't hanging on his every word.

Oh man, Cruz wasn't wrong. Jonathan *was* a sucker for a woman who needed him. And Hartley Farren did. The depth of her need rolled off of her, calling to something deep and fundamental inside him. The same something that drew him to sexual dominance, and always had. It wasn't the *dominance*, per se, it was that sexually dominating a partner allowed him to prioritize pleasing his lover—or lovers—in every and any way they needed. And even some ways they weren't aware that they needed.

Cruz gave a sigh when he didn't get an answer, and Jonathan could almost see him ruefully shaking his head. "Gimme fifteen." They hung up.

"He'll be over in a few," Jonathan said.

"Wow, okay. Thank you, Jonathan. I can't tell you how much this means to me." She released a deep breath, like she'd been ready for him to tell her no, too. Which only deepened his desire to avoid doing just that. "Wanna wait upstairs? More comfortable…"

"Sure." He followed her to the salon, and they slid into the bench seats at the corner table. "Tell me about your charter business," he said, curious to know more about her.

She smiled. "It's been mine for the last three years, but I've been working on the *Far 'n Away* since I graduated from college. Really, longer than that. My father ran a charter company for as long as I can remember. I helped summers and weekends as much as I could, or he'd let me." There was a wistfulness in her expression that spoke of fond memories—and a little heartache, too. "I offer captain-only and some occasional bareboat charters to a handful of regulars I can trust to treat her right. Everything from day sails to week-long excursions."

Hearing her speak, Jonathan's curiosity about her grew into

respect. Because the kinds of sailing she was talking about involved a lot of responsibility, expertise, and confidence. It meant, on any given charter, she was handling everything from being the perfect tour guide, knowing where to take her clients for great snorkeling or the perfect sunset photos, to training those clients to work as the crew and wrangling them to help with cooking, cleaning, and basic boat handling. All by herself.

"Your father must be proud," he said.

Something flashed through those big brown eyes, just for a moment, before she peered at him. "I think he would've been, but I lost him three years ago. It's just me now."

A rock dropped into Jonathan's gut. When he thought of how close he was to his own parents, even though they lived in California where he'd grown up, it was hard to imagine being without them. "I'm really sorry to hear that, Hartley."

"Thanks," she said, one shoulder rising in a small shrug. "But he gave me all this, you know? This love of the wind and the water. The freedom of gliding over the waves. The ability to pit yourself against the elements and win. I don't know, probably sounds corny."

"Not even a little bit," he rushed to reassure her. Because the words reached right inside him. "I grew up on the water myself. I was a surfer. Did the whole competition circuit and everything. Wasn't half bad." He gave her a wink. "After high school, I went to the Naval Academy, and spent eight years in after commissioning. Then Cruz and I opened A&R. I get *exactly* what you're saying."

"It's funny to think you might've been at Annapolis while I was at the University of Maryland, because our sailing team's fleet operated out of the Sailing Association of Eastport, directly across from the Academy."

He chuckled, enjoying the conversation with her. It was easy to make the eyes of those less into the whole sailing culture glaze over, but it was obvious that she was as into it as he was.

"I was on Navy's sailing team, too. But I'd wager to guess that I passed through the Academy well before you went to College Park." He arched a brow as he looked at her, the topic giving him a convenient way to ask a question a man just didn't come out and ask a woman.

She grinned and gave him a sexy smirk. "Think so, huh? I doubt I'm that much younger than you. I turn thirty-one in four weeks."

Ruefully, he shook his head. "A mere babe. I'm thirty-seven."

"Oh, you *are* old." She broke into a belly laugh that made him grin.

But then he schooled his expression, arched a brow, and gave her his stern Dom voice. Just to test her. "I'm gonna make you pay for that, Hartley Farren."

Her eyes flared and her mouth dropped open, though no words came out. He was dying to *hear* a reaction. Finally, she managed, as something that looked more than flirtatious slid into her gaze. "I think that was supposed to sound threatening, Jonathan Allen, but really it was—"

"Knock, knock," came a voice. Damn Cruz's timing. "Permission to come aboard?"

"Oh!" Hartley said, slipping out of the seat. "Is that your friend?" She rushed up the companionway.

Jonathan followed, his gaze locked to her thighs and her strong calves as she moved in front of him. "That's him."

"Hi," she called out when she hit the deck. "Come aboard, please."

Cruz's expression was all business when he looked at her, but the minute the man looked at him, Jonathan saw the knowing humor in his friend's dark eyes.

"I'm Hartley Farren, thank you for coming so quickly." They shook hands.

"Any friend of Jonathan's is a friend of mine," Cruz said.

"Well, uh, I appreciate that," she said with a little chuckle.

A chuckle that doubled Jonathan's curiosity about what she'd been about to say before they'd been interrupted. That she was intrigued by his playful threat? Tempted? Maybe even turned on? Or perhaps she'd been about to say that his threat only made her want to tease him more.

He could've worked with *any* of that.

And he realized that Hartley appealed to him so much that he wanted the chance.

"So, what are we looking at?" Cruz asked, glancing from her back to Jonathan again.

"Right," she said. "This way."

Ten minutes later, Cruz had seen everything, and Jonathan recognized the expression on the man's face—one that spoke of concern and hesitation. In so many ways, the two of them were perfect business partners. They shared interests, goals, and a vision for the types of boats they wanted to build. And they also complimented one another's strengths—and weaknesses. Whereas Jonathan could go with the flow and think fast on his feet in a crisis, Cruz was organized and a stickler for deadlines, punch lists, and charts. And where Jonathan possessed a natural inclination for taking on charity cases, Cruz was a bit of a hard-ass who had to be won over. It was a good balance, one he could see Cruz struggling with as he stared at the warped woodwork throughout the damaged cabin.

Hartley seemed to sense it, too, because she said, "Maybe I should leave you to speak privately?" Without another word, she disappeared up the companionway.

And Jonathan prepared for the ass-kicking he was no doubt about to receive.

Cruz Ramos turned to his best friend and tried not to throttle him. "*Dude*," he said. "We just signed a contract for an ambitious custom build."

Jonathan grinned, and it was that fucking grin that always got to Cruz. The one his asshole of a best friend *knew* always broke his resolve. "I know. I'll take it on after hours as much as possible."

Wow. After hours was when they usually worked at Blasphemy, the BDSM club they co-owned with a bunch of other kinky motherfuckers. Which meant one thing. "You're interested in her."

Jonathan shrugged with one big shoulder, and Cruz kinda wanted to dunk his own head in the bay for how damn sexy he found the gesture. Well, everything about Jonathan Allen, really. The sexy blond surfer-dude hair. The chiseled jaw. The killer body their scenes at the club allowed him to see really freaking often.

All of which was a problem. Because Jonathan was his best friend. And he was straight. And even if Jonathan hadn't been straight, Cruz's religious family would never accept his bisexuality, and certainly never accept him in a gay relationship. It was why he'd never told them about Blasphemy. And that inability to just be himself—kinks and all—was also why he'd fallen away from his family's church, something about which his parents already disapproved. "I'm interested in getting to know her," Jonathan said.

Cruz pushed away the bullshit that constantly lived in his head where Jonathan was concern and heaved a sigh. "You remember that the last time you explored something with someone outside the lifestyle, it didn't go well, right?"

Jonathan rolled his eyes, clearly not needing—or wanting—the reminder. But Cruz gave it to him anyway, because seeing his friend hurt had sucked ass. On Jonathan's third date with a woman he'd met at a coffee shop, his friend had carefully broached the subject of Blasphemy and his date had *flipped*. Apparently, she hadn't been able to get up from the table at the restaurant where they'd been having dinner fast enough, and hadn't resisted throwing a few choice insults over her shoulder as she did.

The whole thing had sucked for Cruz, too. Because he was constantly torn wanting a man he couldn't have and, therefore, encouraging that man to go for other people, which hurt like hell. It was a lose-fucking-lose proposition.

Jonathan arched a brow. "Of course I remember. But I'm not interested in taking on this work just to get this woman to go out with me, asshole. She runs a business out of this marina, too. It's extending a hand of good-will to a business acquaintance."

Cruz scoffed and crossed his arms, but nearly twenty years of friendship meant that he knew Jonathan had already made up his mind. "Jay," he said, using a nickname Jonathan had picked up at the Academy, "we're probably looking at thirty to fifty hours of labor here. More if the electrical needs rewired."

"Agreed," he said.

"Fine. I hope we don't regret this."

Jonathan grinned. *That* fucking grin. "I don't think we're going to regret it at all. Let's go tell Hartley."

They found her above deck, sitting in the captain's chair at the helm. She rushed to her feet, a hopeful expression on her face. Her *pretty* face, Cruz had to admit. His feelings for Jonathan had never kept Cruz from enjoying women—both when they shared them and when he was with a lady alone. "So, what do you think?"

Jonathan cut his gaze to Cruz, and he gave him a nod. "We're in," Jonathan said. "And we're hopeful we can hit your deadline. We'll put together a proposal and get it to you tonight."

She clasped her hands together and nearly wilted in relief. "Oh, my God, thank you."

"Do I get my certificate now?" Jonathan teased, a playfully sexy expression on his face. Cruz frowned, not following.

"No," she said, an equally playful expression on *her* face. "I thought we determined that you needed something more than that. What should it be? A case of your favorite beer? A home-cooked meal? Chocolate chip cookies every day for a month?"

As Cruz watched their private joke unfold, Jonathan laughed. "No special favors required. It's just good to make a new friend here."

"I can never have too many of those," she said, holding out her hand to Jonathan.

He took it and returned the shake. And Cruz stared, because you didn't share sexual partners with someone they way they often had without being able to read facial expressions, understand silent cues, or anticipate where someone was taking something. And what Cruz saw radiating from Jonathan was crystal clear—interest, desire, banked lust. "To our new friendship then. The three of us."

Grinning, Hartley nodded, then extended her hand to Cruz next. "To our new friendship."

Cruz hesitated for just a second. He had nothing against this woman, not at all. It was just that every time Jonathan met someone, Cruz had to wonder if this was the person to whom he'd lose the man he loved.

Finally, he shook her hand and forced a smile. Because it was what it fucking was. "Sounds good to me."

Chapter 3

THE NEXT EVENING, AND AGAINST his better judgment, Cruz Ramos secured the *Far 'n Away* into the boat cradle at A&R's warehouse-style workshop. An industrial space with soaring ceilings that could accommodate sailboats' tall mainmasts, the new catamaran was the fourth vessel in the space—taking up the last of their work room.

He and Jonathan had invited Hartley to make herself comfortable in the suite of offices and waiting rooms that lined the wall closest to the street side of the workshop. Instead, she stood nearby, clearly anxious, even though she remained far enough back to stay clear of the boat's movement in the traveling hoist. And he got it. He'd be as concerned if it was his own boat.

"All right, we have her in hand," Cruz said, securing the last of the straps.

Hartley released a deep breath, and her shoulders fell. "Thank you. Both of you," she added when Jonathan came around from the cat's stern and joined them.

"We're happy to help," Jonathan said, giving Hartley a smile that told Cruz that nothing had changed from the day before. The guy was interested. And from a purely physical standpoint,

Cruz got why. Hartley Farren was sexy in a pretty, all-natural kinda way. She went light on the make-up and seemed perfectly comfortable in her skin, the kind of person who knew who she was so fundamentally that everything she said and did came off with sincerity.

Cruz could appreciate that, too.

And he also got that it wasn't every day they met a woman who shared so wholeheartedly so many of their interests. Except, probably not *all* of their interests.

Therein lay the rub that worried him most.

Their long-term friendship meant neither of them could hide their weaknesses from the other. And Jonathan Allen had a bigger, softer heart than most men Cruz knew. It was a killer combination—that big heart and a Dominant's need to take care. Sometimes, though, it made his partner vulnerable.

Cruz worried this was gonna be one of those times.

On the other hand, if things didn't work out, that meant that much longer that Cruz would have Jonathan to himself. And wasn't he the giant asshole that even a part of him would hope for that.

"We'll start the cabin demo first thing in the morning," Cruz said, attempting to force his brain to focus on the work, "then we'll have a better handle on what we're facing."

Hartley nodded. "Okay, that sounds great. Can I treat you guys to dinner as a token of appreciation? Because by taking this on so fast, you're saving my life right now. You really are."

Cruz smiled, appreciating the gesture. "No, that's not necessary—"

"We'd love to," Jonathan said at the same time.

Hartley turned dark eyes back to him. And man, that hopeful, almost pleading gaze was beguiling and damn hard to deny.

Chuffing out a laugh, he caved. "Okay, then. I could eat."

They ended up at one of his favorite places—a local burger joint with amazing food, a wide range of cold beers on tap, and awesome milkshakes to satisfy his perennial sweet tooth. They made small talk about the menu, and then after they placed their orders, Cruz asked, "So, why the name *Far 'n Away*?" As sailboat names went, it was a good one. Unique without being cutesy. And he was always curious to hear the stories behind boat names.

"Oh," Hartley said with a slow smile. "Well, my dad always used to say that he was far and away happier on the water than anywhere else. So when he opened the charter business and bought his first yacht, I suggested the name, complete with the apostrophe because I thought it was so clever that it was similar to Farren, our last name." She shrugged and pulled a face. "Of course, I was about eight so I guess that was what counted for cleverness back then."

The self-deprecation was charming. He had to admit that. "Well, now I like the name even more," he said.

"It's a great name for a boat, and an even better sentiment," Jonathan said, raising his beer bottle. "To finding that kind of happiness."

Eyeing his best friend with a whole lotta thoughts he could never voice, Cruz raised his bottle as Hartley said, "I'll definitely drink to that." She tapped her ginger ale glass to their beers. And even though she had a smile on her face, something more reserved, maybe even a little sad, flashed behind those big brown eyes. There were layers to this woman Cruz hadn't seen right away. Layers he...appreciated.

He wondered if there were even more he might yet find—if he went digging.

So he did. "Jonathan mentioned you were under a three-week deadline for getting the work done, but didn't say why. Mind if I ask?"

"Not at all. First, because I bought a vendor space at the big sailboat show in Annapolis for the charter business. And second, because I'm teaching in the Sailing University program right after the show ends. I can't do either without the cat, obviously, and both bring charter reservations for next year and income I need for the winter."

Cruz nodded. Even though the Chesapeake tended to have milder winters, boat chartering was unquestionably a business with a seasonal cycle to it.

"And what are you teaching at Sailing University?" Jonathan asked, taking a drink of his beer.

"A 'sailing women' course taught *by* women *for* women; a course on newbie cruiser mistakes; and a course on exploring the Chesapeake Bay. This will be my fourth year teaching, and the first time I've done more than one session, so I'm really looking forward to it." Hartley's eyes were alive with excitement and passion as she spoke, revealing that Cruz had in fact found more layers—a savvy businesswoman, a person who prioritized keeping her commitments, a teacher with expertise that the prestigious Sailing University recognized in having her back year after year.

His effort to resist her appeal was declining minute by minute, especially when Jonathan kept giving him meaningful *I told you so* looks that Cruz could read only too well.

And the conversation they had after their food came didn't help, either. Because Hartley was funny and interesting and sarcastic and even a little flirtatious, and he liked all of those things. He liked them a lot.

And it was clear Jonathan did, too.

But whether Jonathan potentially wanted this woman for himself, or wanted her for the two of them together, one big problem remained in the way—they were Dominants. And they had no idea what Hartley might think of that.

After the string of days stressing over the fate of her boat and her business, Hartley couldn't believe she was having so much fun tonight. But she was. Jonathan and Cruz were great. Jonathan was funny and talkative and so easy going that she couldn't help but feel comfortable with him, even as damn hot as the man was. Though Cruz had seemed more reserved toward her at first, she really appreciated the sincere interest with which he asked her questions, how attentive he was while she talked, and his darker, drier sense of humor. And, God help her, but Cruz was every bit as sexy as Jonathan. Cruz had short black hair, dark eyes, and golden-brown skin. Tattoos peeked out from under the sleeves of his shirt, and he had a hint of a Latin accent.

Sitting between them all night, Hartley's belly had done more than a few flip-flops, because it had been a long time since she'd had dinner with one hot guy, let alone two.

Not that she was *with* either of them, of course. But still, it didn't hurt for a girl to imagine, to wonder, to fantasize…

Nor did it hurt to make new friends when, for so long since her dad's death, Hartley had closed herself off to new relationships of pretty much every kind. She couldn't deny that. She didn't *want* to deny that, not anymore.

So why *not* let herself have a little fun?

"Dessert?" Cruz asked, pulling a plastic menu from behind the napkin holder. "This place has killer milkshakes."

Hartley laughed and rubbed her belly. "You should've told me that before I polished off the whole burger and most of my fries."

"That never matters to Cruz," Jonathan said, smirking. "He has a second stomach reserved for dessert."

Cruz nodded. "Pretty much."

Chuckling, Hartley enjoyed the men's good-natured teasing. It was clear how close they were, and she guessed that made sense since they not only operated a business together, but had served in the navy together, too.

"We should all be so lucky," she said.

"What flavors do you like? I'll get one and you can have some." He leveled that intense, dark gaze on her.

And her belly did that silly flipping thing again. The weird thing wasn't that Cruz's gaze had the ability to do that to her, it was that her belly seemed to react that way to *both* of them. Sure proof that it had been too long since she'd last been with a man.

"You should take him up on that, Hartley. This is a man who never shares his sweets." Jonathan winked.

She grinned, because it seemed like there was something more to his words and that wink. "Is that right?"

Cruz arched a brow at his friend before looking to her again and nodding. "Hardly ever."

"I feel special then."

"You should," he said flashing her a sexy smile.

Annnd *belly flip*.

"Well, all righty," she said with a nervous chuckle. "I mean, obviously chocolate is the best milkshake ever. But Oreo is pretty good, and I like strawberry, too. But no vanilla, I'm sorry to say. You might as well just drink milk."

Slowly but surely, the most amused expression drew up over Cruz's darkly masculine features. "You don't like vanilla."

"No, it's totally boring."

"Boring," he repeated, that amused expression growing until he looked like he might bust out laughing.

She glanced at Jonathan and found him fighting back humor himself. Why were they— "Oh, God, it's your favorite, isn't it?"

Deep laughter finally broke free from Cruz, causing his eyes to crinkle at the corners and dimples to form in his cheeks. Jonathan grinned, too, as Cruz managed, "Vanilla is definitely *not* my favorite, Hartley." Still chuckling, he closed the menu and returned it to its slot behind the napkins. "Chocolate it is. But tell me, do you object to whipped cream?"

Still feeling like she'd missed something, Hartley shook her head. "No, whipped cream is awesome. When it comes to milkshakes and hot chocolate, you can never have too much."

Grinning, he nodded. "I'll keep that in mind. I like a woman with such definite opinions about her desserts."

The waitress came just then to clear their plates and take their dessert order. As she stepped away, Hartley noticed three women get up from a table across the dining room. The one who'd had her back to Hartley was immediately recognizable—because of her hip-length black hair that swung in soft waves over gorgeous curves.

When the women turned toward their table to make for the door, Hartley's suspicions were confirmed, and she waved. "Hey, Scarlett." Along with Linda, Scarlett Rose was one of her closest friends. Even so, both of their lives had become so hectic over the past year that they hadn't spent as much time together as they once had. The charter business often pulled Hartley away on weekends when other people socialized, and sometimes took her away for weeks at a time when she had mid-week charters scheduled, too. As much as she loved being out on the word, chartering made staying connected unexpectedly hard.

Her friend did a double take and then was heading their way and smiling with lips painted in her trademark bright red shade. "Hartley, hey. It's so good to see…you…" Her words trailed off as her gaze landed first on Jonathan, and then Cruz. "And, um, hello," she said with a suddenly nervous little laugh.

"Scarlett," Cruz said, nodding his head before rising. "Nice to see you." He offered his hand to Scarlett before smiling at the other two. "Cass. Kenna. You, too. What kind of trouble are the three of you up to tonight?"

The blond woman smirked and answered for the group. "We get to have *some* secrets, don't we?" She planted a hand on her hip, which was when Hartley noticed that her other arm had a prosthesis extending from below the elbow.

Cruz chuckled and shook his head. "Not too many, I hope."

"Hartley, let me make introductions," Jonathan said, rising to join the others. Hartley stood, too, wondering how Scarlett knew the men—and why seeing them had flustered her so. "This is Kenna Sloane," he said. "One of our favorite people in the world to razz because she served in the Marine Corps. But we try not to hold that against her."

The blond woman was gorgeous, but what Hartley really noticed about her was her feisty attitude. "Hi, Hartley. Nice to meet you. Ignore them, though. They're just mad because some people actually got to fight overseas while they went on a cruise."

Hartley laughed. Having lived in the area all her life, she was well familiar with the rivalries that existed between the military services. Both the navy and marines commissioned students out of the Naval Academy, and she'd known more than a few people who attended school there. "Great to meet you, too, Kenna. But count me out of getting in the middle of the age-old conflict."

Kenna winked. "Probably smart. I can handle 'em myself though. Because, marine."

Next to her, a pretty brunette woman laughed. "Hi, Hartley, I'm Cassia. You're wise to stay out of the middle of this because it *never ends*."

Hartley grinned and returned the greeting. "It's great meeting friends of new friends. How do you all know each other?" she asked.

A beat passed. The women looked to the men. Finally, Jonathan answered. "We all belong to a club and see each other fairly frequently."

Why did that sound, at once, perfectly normal and like there was a whole lot more he could've said. Hartley was almost tempted to ask *what club?* But something kept her from voicing the question. "Oh, that's awesome," she said instead. "Scarlett and I have been friends for a while now. What? Four years?"

"Five," Scarlett said. "We met in a cooking class. A class at which Hartley excelled while I've been known to burn toast. Which made it really bad for her because we were put together as partners."

Hartley laughed, remembering that class well. The only thing that had enabled both of them to get through it was the wine, but the experience had forged them as friends. Something both of them had needed and appreciated when Scarlett ended up going through a difficult divorce with a man who'd turned into an abusive asshole, and Hartley's dad had died.

Regret suddenly rolled through Hartley in a slow wave, because she hadn't done anything like that class since her father died. Hadn't tried to learn something new. Hadn't taken a risk. Hadn't put herself out there in any meaningful way.

The waitress arrived with the milkshake, forcing them to all step aside so she could get to the table to put down the huge glass and accompanying separate metal container.

"Well, I hate to break up our little party, but I'm supposed to meet Quinton soon," Cass said. "It was really nice to meet you, Hartley." She smiled as her gaze moved from the men back to her. "Hope to see you again."

"Same here," Hartley said.

Scarlett touched her arm. "We need to catch up soon. I have news."

"Of course," Hartley said, hoping it was good news. Scarlett deserved it after everything she'd been through the past few years. "Though how am I supposed to wait to hear it? I'll text you."

Moments later, it was just the three of them, settling into their table once more. And Hartley would've sworn the men shared some sort of meaningful look. But then Cruz was smiling, doling out spoons, and pushing the overflowing treat between them.

"Tell me this isn't one of the best milkshakes you've ever tasted," he said, arching a brow. When Cruz wasn't being reserved and a little broody, he could be charming and sexy as hell.

Smiling, Hartley tried a spoonful. And as the cold, rich sweetness exploded on her tongue, she couldn't help but moan. "Oh, my God," she said, hand in front of her mouth as she finished swallowing the bite. She took another. "No one has ever been more right about anything."

The sexiest smile she'd ever seen from any man slid up his handsome face, and he pointed his spoon at her. "I like you, Hartley. You're good people."

"Let me in there," Jonathan said playfully, diving in with his own spoon. "You two don't get to have all the fun." He banged against her spoon with his like he was trying to swat it out of the way.

Hartley laughed. "Simmer down, Jonathan." She knocked the ice cream off his spoon and stole it, bursting into laughter as his mouth dropped open and she swallowed down the sweet cream.

He leaned closer. So close that her breath caught. "I promise you this, Hartley Farren. Somehow. Someway. You're going to pay for that."

She arched a brow as her heart tripped into a sprint and tingles erupted over her skin. Because the way those words hit her almost like a caress that proved Jonathan Allen gave good flirt. "You keep threatening that…"

He leaned in closer. "I'll have my revenge, darlin'. Count on it."

Chapter 4

THE NEXT DAY, JONATHAN WAS knee deep in interior demolition of Hartley's catamaran, Cruz working right beside him. They had to be gentle in tearing out the damaged wood so that they didn't create new damage in the tight quarters. Luckily, the larger hole they'd cut in the hull's fiberglass helped with that particular problem.

They wouldn't know exactly how much this job would cost or how long it would take until they determined the condition of the electrical system. If the collision and water had damaged that, the repairs were a whole other ballgame.

He really hoped for Hartley's sake that wasn't the case.

Thinking of her had him smiling. The way her eyes had flared when he'd leaned in and issued his playful threat. The way her mouth had dropped open, sweet and kissable. The way Cruz had slowly but surely warmed to Hartley. Jonathan had been able to see it in his friend's eyes, hear it in his words, and read it in his body language. Twenty years of friendship gave you that ability.

"Any chance you're gonna stop daydreaming?" Cruz said, amusement plain in his tone.

"Some people can walk and chew gum at the same damn

time, asshole," Jonathan shot back with a smirk as he tossed a section of warped wood out the hole.

Cruz rolled his eyes.

"Don't tell me your mind isn't on her, too." Jonathan nailed the other man with a stare.

Cruz pulled another section of wood free and for a long moment didn't reply. Then he stood upright and returned that stare. "What is it you want with Hartley, man?"

"It's damn early to want anything, specifically."

Arching a dark brow that called him on his shit all by itself, Cruz didn't let it go at that. "Yeah, it is. But that doesn't mean you don't have an idea."

Jonathan dropped the tool he'd been using and braced his hands on his hips. "Okay, fine. I want to get to know her enough to see if she might be as great as she seems. To see if she might share even more interests in common."

"You're *that* into her already?"

"Maybe. Okay, probably." It was crazy fast to be admitting that, let alone feeling it. Jonathan knew it was. But there was just something about her that had its hooks in him—just from the couple days they'd spent together. She was funny and interesting and smart, and all of that was in addition to their shared love of being out on the water. That had been fundamental to who Jonathan was going back to his childhood. More than a decade in the military taught him to listen to his instincts and trust his gut, and his gut was telling him there could be something worth exploring. "What about you?"

"Me?"

"Yeah, you. You interested, too?" he asked. Because though they hadn't always shared sexual partners, they'd been doing it more and more. The first time it'd happened, it'd been totally organic. They'd met a woman at a club. Had great conversation. Danced with her. And then she'd invited them to come home with her. Both of them.

It had been a night that'd blown their minds. The thrill of it. The intensity. The courage it took to bare yourself in front of not just one lover, but two. In those early years, they'd both had plenty of solo dates and relationships, but they'd met more and more women who were open to sharing, and a few who introduced them to the BDSM lifestyle, where ménage scenarios were more accepted, common, and available.

It had cracked something open inside of Jonathan, something that needed to please, to take care, to love, and that felt too big to share with just one person. It was hard to articulate, and that was the closest he'd ever been able to come to explaining it—even to himself. Cruz was more private about what it meant to him—which Jonathan got given how religious his family was—but one thing was clear: they'd been through so much together by the time they'd found the lifestyle that they could trust each other, implicitly, in being themselves, both in and out of the bedroom. No questions, no judgment.

And then they'd met Hale O'Keeffe, Isaac Marten, Quinton Ross, and the other men who, with them, would become co-owners and the Master Dominants of Blasphemy, Baltimore's most exclusive BDSM club.

That was when not just playing at this lifestyle, but truly *living* it, first became more than a possibility.

Cruz released a deep breath. "You…you don't want her just for yourself?" His voice was quiet in the confined space of the ruined cabin. And Jonathan didn't think he was imagining almost a…regret in his tone.

He stepped closer and squeezed his friend's shoulder. "We've talked about this before, yeah? If the right woman, the right situation, presented itself…" Jonathan let the words hang there. "I'm thinking, maybe we've found her. Especially now that we know she's long-time friends with a woman who's a submissive at the club. That shit didn't feel like a coincidence."

His friend's gaze was dark and intense, and suddenly flared

with a heat Jonathan had seen in the other man's eyes many times. The heat of interest. *Hell, yeah.* Jonathan smiled, because Cruz *was* on board. This wasn't just him getting caught up all on his own.

Cruz swallowed hard, and the sound was thick and a little tortured. "Maybe we have found the right woman."

"Then you're in on seeing where this might go?"

"I'm in, Jonathan."

Satisfaction stirred in his gut. "Good."

"But the fact that Hartley knows Scarlett doesn't mean she also knows Scarlett's a submissive. Or even what that fully means." Cruz arched a dark brow.

Jonathan nodded, allowing him that much. "True. But maybe she does. And if so, that could be useful."

Cruz's expression went thoughtful, his gaze distant. "It would certainly make broaching the whole topic of BDSM easier if she already knew about the lifestyle."

"Damn straight," Jonathan said, grinning.

"Then I say we find out from Scarlett exactly what Hartley knows." His friend's dark brown eyes narrowed as his mind turned the situation over and looked at it from all angles. That methodical, analytical mind made Cruz an excellent sailor, a fantastic business partner, and an intriguing lover. Many times, Jonathan had witnessed Cruz drive a partner crazy with the workings of his mind as much as with the touch of his hands.

"Now you're thinking," Jonathan said. "That's exactly where we start."

Hartley found Scarlett sitting in the late September sunshine at an outdoor table of a cafe where they'd planned to meet for lunch. "I took the liberty of ordering us some wine. Mind sitting outside?" Scarlett asked, rising to give Hartley a hug. Her friend wore a pair of hip-hugging jeans and a royal blue wrap shirt—all of which highlighted her hourglass shape.

"Not at all. It's gorgeous today." She slipped into her seat and smoothed the white linen napkin over her own jeans. "It's been too long since we did this. I'm glad I ran into you the other night."

"I agree," Scarlett said, adjusting the twist of her long, black hair over her shoulder. She had the most gorgeous hair of anyone Hartley knew. Like black silk. "To you, sister."

"Right back atcha," Hartley said.

Smiling, they toasted and then made small talk as they decided and finally ordered a bread-and-fresh-mozzarella appetizer and salads for lunch. And then Scarlett leaned forward. "Okay, I literally don't know where to start." The big smile she wore encouraged Hartley that Scarlett's news was good.

"Well, start at the beginning, woman. What's your news?" She sipped at her chardonnay, crisp and bright.

Scarlett waved her hands. "No, no. We're not starting there. We're starting with Jonathan and Cruz."

Hartley blinked. She'd absolutely planned to ask more about how Scarlett knew the heroes saving her life by taking on her boat repair so quickly, but that hadn't been why her friend had asked her to lunch. "Uh. Well…" She chuckled, because Scarlett looked like she might burst with excitement. What the heck was that about? "I hired them to repair the *Far 'n Away*. It got damaged in the hurricane last week and my friend, Linda, introduced me to Jonathan. He agreed to take a look when no one else was available. Which was a lifesaver because I have commitments lined up in a few weeks that would kill me to miss."

Now Scarlett was the one blinking as she swallowed a drink of wine. "And?"

"And what?"

"You guys looked very flirtatious." Scarlett arched a brow.

"Flirtatious? With which one?" Hartley asked, trying to

remember what they'd been talking about when she'd noticed Scarlett at the restaurant.

"Hon, with *both* of them."

"Oh, my God, no!" Hartley laughed, nearly choking on the drink she'd just taken. "We're just friends. New friends, at that. I don't even know them that well."

"Well, I guessed that much," she said, her tone full of innuendo.

She sat forward in her seat. "Okay, what does *that* mean? What is this club where you're all members?"

"We're gonna need another round of wine for this conversation," Scarlett said, holding up her hand and gesturing to their half-full glasses when she caught the waiter's eye.

"Oh, God," Hartley said, putting her hand to her head. "Do I even want to know?"

"Trust me," Scarlett said. "You do."

Taking a deep breath, she nodded. "Okay, hit me."

Scarlett's expression was alive with amusement. "Do you remember the club I talked to you about? The, um—" Her voice dropped into a whisper. "—BDSM club? The one you encouraged me to go for it and join?"

One beat passed, then another. "*That's* the club you all belong to?" She took a long gulp of her chardonnay as her friend nodded.

Scarlett had told her about the club after her divorce had been finalized. Her husband hadn't been happy at all when Scarlett had expressed a desire to explore the more risqué sides of her sexuality, and he'd become so cruel to her for revealing what truly interested her that she'd been forced to leave him. Hartley had been only too happy to cheer her friend on when she'd discovered the existence of this club and tell her she had nothing to lose by giving it a try. As far as Hartley was concerned, anything two consenting adults agreed to do was no one else's business.

Scarlett gave her a long moment to process that news before she continued. "Yup. That's the club. Blasphemy. You know that dance club called Club Diablo over in the warehouse district?"

"Yeah."

"You actually go through that club to get to Blasphemy. It's located in a restored church behind that building. You wouldn't know it's there without knowing about the club, which is kinda the point. They're very private and exclusive, for obvious reasons." The waiter arrived and filled Hartley's now much less full glass.

Hartley took another big sip and tried to make sense of her thoughts. "Okay, so, what? Are they like you?"

"A submissive, you mean?" When Hartley nodded, Scarlett said, "No. They're Dominants. They like to control the scenes and their partners' pleasure. Master Jonathan and Master Cruz are alphas through and through." Scarlett gave her a teasing smirk.

"Master..." Hartley murmured, trying out the word. Aided by her friend's commentary, her brain offered up *all kinds* of unhelpful imaginings. Her, on her knees, Jonathan standing over her. Or would it be Cruz? Being pulled over one of their laps, her ass in the air, hands stroking her. But whose hand? Gah. This was a full-on trip to crazytown. "Um, okay."

Just then, the waiter arrived with their appetizer, but Hartley was too gobsmacked to think about food. As Scarlett forked a piece of mozzarella onto her plate, she looked like the cat that ate the canary. "There's more."

"How can there be more?" She almost didn't want to know. No, scratch that, she *really* wanted to know. "What kind of more?"

"Take another sip," Scarlett said, chuckling and tapping at the rim of her wine glass.

Hartley didn't resist. She took a big drink, her heart racing, her head spinning, just a little, because she'd skipped breakfast this morning.

"Hartley, Jonathan and Cruz do scenes together."

"Oh." Her shoulders fell. "So they're a couple?" Man, that was…kinda disappointing. She totally got it, though. They were beautiful men. Best friends. Had served in the military together and now were business partners. It made sense that they could be together romantically. But, damn, she'd read that flirtation all wrong, hadn't she?

And hell if that disappointment she was feeling didn't reveal a thing or two…

Scarlett shook her head. "No, well, maybe. I don't know. There's some speculation around the club that there might be something romantic between them. But what I mean is, they do scenes together. Both of them with the same submissive. At one time. You know, like, *ménage à trois*."

It was a good thing Hartley had just swallowed, because otherwise she might've done a cartoon-like spit take. Heat roared through her body. Because those imaginings she'd just done… that question she'd just asked herself about which one would be starring in those fantasies with her…*now* she had her answer. They might not make her choose.

"That is the…hottest, craziest thing I've ever heard in my whole life," Hartley managed, her brain possibly shorting out at the thought. *Both* of them. Together. At the same time. Jonathan's golden-boy good looks. Cruz's dark, intensity. At. The. Same. Time.

Scarlett burst out laughing. "Hot, for sure. I've seen them do a scene together, and trust me when I say, *no one* complains afterward." She waggled her eyebrows. "But it's not as crazy as you think. After the last year of exploring things in my own life, I can tell you that there's a whole culture out there—both within the BDSM lifestyle and outside of it—that's a lot more open-minded and fluid."

For a long moment, they sat quietly and enjoyed bites of the warm, smooth mozzarella, tangy tomatoes, and flavorful pieces of basil atop crostini.

"But...I don't think I'm submissive," Hartley said. "I mean, how do you even know?" And then she shook her head, peered around at the other diners to see if anyone was eavesdropping, and dropped her voice to a whisper. "And that's all beside the fact that I'm not sure I'd be brave enough to try being with two men at once."

Scarlett gave her an appraising look. "First of all, you're not ruling it out, and that already tells me you're more open-minded than the average bear." She winked. "And, second, and you don't have to tell me the answer, but imagine being with them both and ask yourself if the idea turns you on."

Hartley swallowed hard as goosebumps raced across her skin. The attention of two men at once. Two pairs of hands. Two mouths. Two...other things. Had it gotten warmer outside?

"Actually, you really don't have to tell me, my friend, because I just saw it in your eyes." There was a little teasing in her tone, but mostly Scarlett's expression was full of understanding.

Blowing out a long breath, Hartley chuckled. "Okay, well, I have no idea what to do with any of that. Especially since it's not like they've asked me for anything. So maybe we should talk about your news now."

Scarlett grinned. "Okay, I won't push. But let me just say this one last thing. If you decide you might be curious, there's a masquerade party at the club in a few weeks. Masks required. You could just observe if you wanted. You wouldn't have to participate. I could get you in on my membership. All you'd have to do is fill out a few forms."

Actually *attend* a BDSM club? Hartley's racing heart told her that, at the very least, the idea excited her. Even if some of that excitement was fear. "I'll think about it."

Scarlett nodded. "Okay. So, then, my news is that I've gotten a job offer. And I'm not sure whether to take it."

"Wow!" Hartley said. Scarlett worked as a statistician and was beyond brilliant. The sexiest math nerd on the planet, probably. "Congratulations. Where's the job?"

"That's the thing," she said. "It's in Vegas."

Hartley blinked, instantly torn between happiness for her friend and regret for herself. "Vegas, how exciting. I imagine there's a lot of opportunity in the casinos for people who can work numbers the way you can."

"Exactly," she said. "And I'm thinking…maybe a move would be a way to put the pain of everything that happened with my ex behind me."

The very idea of Scarlett moving felt like another in a long line of losses. Not having a mother. Her dad's heart attack. Her grandmother's dementia. But this wasn't about Hartley, and her friend deserved every iota of happiness she could find. "I don't think it sounds like you're undecided, Scarlett. To me it sounds like you just want confirmation that this is the right thing to do. And your voice and face are telling me that it is. You deserve a fresh start after what he put you through." And Hartley meant it. She really did. Even though Scarlett's absence would leave another hole in her life.

"Really? You don't think it's, I don't know, rash to just pick up and move across the country?"

"Not in the least," Hartley said. "And not for nothing, but you just got done encouraging me to consider a relationship with two men at the same time. Who, by the way, may or may not be interested in me in the first place."

They laughed.

"I think…I think this could be good for me, you know?" Scarlett said, just barely holding back her excitement. "I'm still thinking it through, though."

Hartley hoped Scarlett wasn't restraining her enthusiasm for her sake, though Hartley wouldn't put it past her. Scarlett was one of the few people with whom Hartley had ever shared her loneliness. After Scarlett's divorce, it was something they'd had in common. So Hartley made sure her voice bubbled over with encouragement. "Well, it sounds like a great opportunity. I'm so proud of you, Scarlett. And I promise I'll come visit."

The waiter delivered their salads, which they ate around one of the liveliest, most animated lunches Hartley had had in a long time. And even though a part of her was already missing her friend, she had to respect the courage it took Scarlett to identify the kind of life she really wanted and go after it, no matter what anyone else thought.

Right at that moment, Hartley wished she could be more like that.

Chapter 5

Hartley woke up surrounded by skin. Miles of warm, smooth skin. Hard muscles as far as her hands could reach.

It was freaking delicious.

"Good morning, beautiful," Jonathan said, kissing her ear, her neck, her shoulder. His hand slid around low on her belly, his long fingers tantalizingly close to where she knew he could drive her wild.

"Good morning," she murmured dreamily, a moan spilling from her throat when he rocked his hips and pressed his rock-hard cock against her ass.

"Mmm, I think she likes whatever you're doing under these covers," Cruz said from right in front of her. He burrowed closer, his thigh pushing between hers, his firm muscles providing a sudden, blindingly good friction as he claimed her mouth.

Hartley had never been more turned on in her life.

She allowed herself to be pulled on top of Cruz, straddling him even though he was the one in control. He took firm hold of her hips and forced her to grind her clit against the hard ridge of his length. She was already so wet that her own lubrication made them both slick, driving her mad with urgent need.

"Tell us how much you love having both of us, Hartley," Jonathan whispered as he shifted to his knees behind her. His hands stroked down her spine, and his explorations ended with his hand behind her thighs, a finger sinking deep into her pussy.

"Oh, God. I do," she rasped.

"Fuck," Cruz bit out, his darkly handsome face painted with arousal of his own. "Put me inside you, Hartley."

Rising up a little, Hartley took his thick length in hand, and then sank down onto it inch by heart-stopping inch.

"Goddamn, that looks good," Jonathan said behind her. His hands fell on her shoulders and pressed her down until she'd taken in all of the man beneath her. Then his touch fell away, and was replaced by the wet sound of friction. A hand moving slick and repeatedly over skin.

Jonathan was preparing himself for her. Then his lubed fingers were at her rear, preparing her for him.

Her forehead dropped to Cruz's when Jonathan inserted first one, then two fingers. She'd only done this a few times before, but it had been a couple of years, and she'd never done it with two men.

"I'll go slow," Jonathan was saying. "I'll make you feel so good."

"We both will," Cruz promised, claiming her mouth in a kiss again.

And then the head of Jonathan's cock was right there. Lined up and invading her most intimate space.

On a gasp, Hartley's eyes blinked open...and she found herself alone. In her bed, with the gray light of early morning peaking around her blinds. Lying almost all the way on her stomach except for the way her thigh was thrown across a pillow. And she was more aroused than she'd ever been in her life.

From a dream

From a *sex* dream.

A sex dream where she had sex with two men at once. And not just *any* men. Jonathan and Cruz.

And knowing it had only been a dream did absolutely nothing to make her less aroused.

"Holy shit," she whispered, flopping onto her back and almost desperate for some sort of release.

She debated for less than a second, then reached for her laptop, which she'd stowed on her nightstand before she'd gone to bed. It didn't take long to navigate to the porn site she sometimes visited. After all, a woman had needs. And a woman not in a relationship had to fulfill those needs all by herself.

What she wanted to come to wasn't even a question. She typed one word into the search bar: *threesome*

And, the porn gods were apparently smiling on her, because it only took until the second screen of results to find a twenty-minute-long clip starring men who bore some physical resemblance to the two men who'd starred in her dream. A tall, longer-haired blond. And a muscular black-haired Latino.

The way she felt, there was no way in hell Hartley was going to need twenty minutes.

She propped the laptop up on a pillow, fast forwarded past the obligatory blow-job scene, and pressed play as the men pushed the woman onto a bed.

Hartley's heart already hammered in her chest. She threw off the covers, kicked off her panties, and reached between her legs to find herself wet. But that was just what her dream had done to her.

Now, as her fingers started to move, her gaze latched onto the actors on the screen. They were all over the woman. One man fucking her mouth, while the other man pushed his head between her legs. Now they were positioning her between them, just as Jonathan and Cruz had done in her dream. And then she was about to be filled with both of their cocks, one in her pussy, one in her ass.

The instant the second man penetrated the rosebud of the actress's rear, Hartley came on a gasping cry. Her fingers swirled harder, faster, drawing out the pulses of her orgasm until Hartley was limp and incredulous. She wasn't sure she'd ever come harder in her whole life.

For a long moment, she stared blankly up at her bedroom ceiling.

It was just a dream. It was just a fantasy. It wasn't real life at all. Right?

Well, it wasn't *her* real life. But according to Scarlett, it was Jonathan and Cruz's.

Could it also be hers? Would she be brave enough to do such a thing if the men ever offered?

Doubts and questions ran through her mind. Was it possible that Jonathan and Cruz even thought of her this way? And if so, what would people think? Would they *tell* people? What if she got freaked out part way through? Would it hurt to have two men at the same time? (She wasn't sure, but her brain sure was trying to convince her she should at least give it a try…)

Beep beep beep…

Rolling, Hartley smacked at the LED screen of her phone to turn off her alarm.

And then she forced herself out of bed and into the shower. Because despite having just come to just the *idea* of sleeping with her new friends, she had to see them in less than two hours. And somehow she was going to have to figure out how to act normal when she did.

Jonathan disconnected from his phone call with Scarlett Rose and grinned at Cruz, sitting on the corner of his desk. "She knows," Jonathan said. "They had lunch yesterday and Scarlett told her."

A slow smile quirked the corner of Cruz's mouth. "Remind me to think up a really big gift for Scarlett."

"Right?" Jonathan said. "And better yet, Scarlett said Hartley seemed open to the idea."

Cruz crossed his arms, emphasizing how jacked his shoulders were. Not surprising when, every single morning, the guy hit the gym in the condo complex where they both owned units. At least three or four mornings a week, Jonathan met him there, but he preferred to pound out five miles on the treadmill rather than lift. "Which idea exactly?"

Jonathan sat forward, his arms resting on the desk top and his hands tapping out a little beat. "*All* of it. Trying out the club. Us being Doms. The fact that we're into ménage."

Cruz rubbed the back of his neck. "Jesus."

"Is that a good Jesus or a bad Jesus?" Jonathan asked, wondering where his friend's head was at.

Chuckling, Cruz shrugged. "I'm hoping it's a good one. But I think we gotta let this develop naturally. We try to force this thing and we could scare her off."

Nodding, Jonathan said, "Roger that. But it's a huge help that she was at least clued into the lifestyle through Scarlett, who, by the way, mentioned the masquerade party to her."

Cruz's eyes went wide. "Seriously. A big present. Huge."

"We will," Jonathan said, laughing.

They'd barely finished the conversation when they heard a voice from out on the workshop floor. "Knock knock?"

Jonathan grinned and rounded the desk. "Hey, we're in here," he called. Cruz followed him out of the suite of offices. They found Hartley standing in the big space, a ray of sunshine in the dimness of the gray morning, dressed in a sexy pair of low-riding jeans and a pretty yellow boat-necked shirt that framed the graceful slope of her neck and collarbones. Today she'd styled her hair down in big, loose curls that extended to her breasts. She was fucking beautiful. "Nice to see you, Hartley. How are you?"

She smiled as she met his gaze. "I'm great. Especially since I get to see my baby again." She nodded toward the *Far 'n Away*.

Cruz flashed a wicked grin. "We'll try not to get our feelings hurt that you're more excited to see the boat than us."

Hartley blushed a beautiful, bright pink. One that made all three of them laugh. "That's not what I meant," she insisted. And it was as endearing as it was intriguing, because both the color and her words seemed to indicate that she didn't want them to think she wasn't happy to see them, too.

"Come on. Let us show you what's happening," Jonathan said, leading their little group to the cat. "The good news is, the electrical is fine."

"Oh, thank God," Hartley said, her hands going to her heart.

He nodded, really freaking happy for her. Because that reality saved her thousands of dollars and several weeks' worth of down time. They would've been seriously hard-pressed to meet her deadline if the catamaran had needed rewired.

"It's good news, for sure," Cruz said. "Now we need your input on what patching technique you'd like us to use for the hole in the hull, whether you want the whole bottom repainted to hide the patch, and which wood grain you want us to use on the interior."

Jonathan nodded. "We have a few that are close, but it's impossible to exactly match either the grain or the stain."

Hartley dropped her little purse to the floor next to a beam. "Okay, show me what you need."

An hour later, they'd walked through everything, and Hartley had made all the decisions. The three of them were squeezed into the narrow space of the cabin, where she stood staring at the skeleton of the space. "I know it's going to be fine, but it's really hard seeing her like this. It's just a boat, of course, but I bought this catamaran with my father's life insurance as a way to build up the business that had faltered in his absence. So, in a weird way, this boat…has always felt like it's the last part of him I have left. I know that sounds ridiculous…" Suddenly, she rapidly blinked her eyes as her breath caught. "Sorry."

"Damn, Hartley. It doesn't sound ridiculous at all," Jonathan said, opening his arms. "Come here."

She hesitated for only a second, and then she folded herself in against his chest.

...and burrowed right into Jonathan's heart.

Over her head, he met Cruz's gaze and found it burning with the same connection Jonathan was starting to feel. "The fact that she's so special to you makes us feel even more privileged to get to take care of her for you, you know?"

She nodded and swiped her fingers under her eyes, though she didn't pull away. "My mom died of a stroke when I was four. I don't have any first-hand memories of her at all. And even though it was sad not to have a mother, my dad was so great that I never felt like I didn't have what I needed. Until he died."

Damn. She was all alone.

Cruz placed a comforting hand on her shoulder and squeezed. "I'm sorry to hear that, Hartley. My family is big and in each other's business constantly, so I can't imagine what all of that was like. Even though, occasionally, it might be nice for there to be fewer busy-bodies floating around the edges of my life."

She chuckled. "Well, yeah, I can imagine…"

Her sentiment was perfectly normal, but her tone possessed more than a little innuendo. A sudden tension ballooned inside the tiny space. Because, for exactly what reason did she imagine Cruz might want privacy? Given what they'd learned she knew, one reason came immediately to mind.

And a metaphorical door swung open…

"Thanks," she whispered, finally stepping back from Jonathan. Right away, he missed her warmth and her softness and her sweetness. She gave them both a shaky smile.

"Hartley," Jonathan said gently, pushing that door open just a little further. "I want to say something but you are more than welcome to tell me you don't want to discuss it."

Her gaze slowly lifted to his. "Um. Okay?" Color slowly crept into her cheeks again.

Cruz flashed him a look, but Jonathan wasn't going to push *too* hard. "We talked to Scarlett this morning."

Her eyes went wide and she shivered. Just a little tremor, but one that revealed she knew exactly what they'd discussed. As interesting, the mere mention of that knowledge made her have an intriguing visceral reaction. "Oh." She crossed her arms over her chest.

Jonathan gave her a smile. "Yeah." She glanced at Cruz, her blush spreading down her throat. And it was everything Jonathan could do not to pull her back into his arms. Or into his lap. Anything to bring her closer again, especially as he broached this topic. "I just wanted to invite you to ask us any questions you might have, any time you like."

A fast nod. A little smile. Quick, peaking glances at Jonathan, then Cruz, then the deck between them. All of which communicated a little embarrassment, perhaps, but no distaste, no disapproval. Perfect.

Cruz was the one to break the tension. "So, we'll get started ordering the materials, and hopefully we'll have what we need on hand within two days."

"That sounds perfect," Hartley said, clearing her throat. " And I want you to know I'm available to help. I do a lot of my own maintenance, so I'm relatively handy. My dad made sure of that. And, uh, I don't have much to do since I've had to cancel my charters. So I'm happy to be put to work." The words spilled out in a nervous rush.

Jonathan smiled, appreciating that she was willing to pitch in, especially given that they'd squeezed in her job. But they hadn't taken on more than they could handle. Still, he nailed her with a stare and said, "You're welcome here any time."

"Absolutely," Cruz said, stepping just a little closer. And Jonathan could see the same battle being waged in his friend's eyes.

The battle against touching her, holding her, showing how good they could make her feel. It fueled Jonathan's own need. "Consider our door open to you, Hartley. Day or night. All you have to do is walk through it."

Chapter 6

Driving home from yet another day of helping work on her catamaran—today she'd assisted with preparing the bottom of the boat for the eventual repainting it would need—Hartley's cell phone rang through the Bluetooth in her car.

Scarlett's name popped up on the caller ID, and she smiled even as her heart gave a little pang.

"Hi, Scarlett."

"Hey, girl, how are you?"

"I'm good. Well, honestly, I'm a little tired. I've been pitching in with the *Far 'n Away* as much as Jonathan and Cruz will let me. And the stress of whether we're going to finish in time for the sailboat show is starting to wake me up at night."

"Aw, honey, I'm sorry to hear that. Are they making good progress?" Scarlett asked.

"Yes, they're busting their butts. And their work is first-rate. I'm just a stress bucket."

Scarlett chuckled. "With good reason. But I might have news that will at least offer a distraction."

"Oh, do tell," Hartley said, a grin crawling up her face as she braked at a traffic light. Fortunately, with how often she went back and forth to the marina, her small one-bedroom apartment was only a ten-minute drive away. "Did you accept the job?"

"No, not yet, but I'm seriously thinking about it. They're giving me the hard sell, which is tempting me even more. But that's not my news." There was an undercurrent of excitement to her tone.

"Wait, but a hard sell is good. It means they really want you."

"Yes, I agree. And that feels damn good. But, *girl*, I called because you gotta know. Jonathan and Cruz haven't done a single scene at Blasphemy since they met you. And they've even rearranged their schedules to have others cover their shifts."

As Hartley pulled the car into her parking space and shut off the engine, she wasn't sure which part of that to respond to first. "Wait, what shifts?"

"They don't just belong to Blasphemy, Hart. They're two of the twelve Master Dominants who co-own the club. And they all take turns running it."

"What? When do they do that?" Her thoughts scrambled and a shiver ran over her skin. Of excitement? Awe? Surprise? Because, they *owned* a BDSM club? They were *Master Dominants*? There was no question that some part of her liked thinking of them in those terms given the tingling that ran right down her center. "But…they're always at A&R." Including all day today, a Saturday. A thing that she'd appreciated so much, because they'd both downplayed it as if it were totally normal.

"Blasphemy's an after-hours club. It doesn't even open until seven most nights. But they switched with other Doms to cover for them tonight, which is why Kenna called me to see what was going on. Because apparently, everyone's speculating on why they're not playing and where they've been. And that's why I'm calling you." She said this like she was revealing a spy network that traded in state secrets.

"Oh," Hartley murmured, blinking into the darkness of the parking lot. It was almost nine o'clock now, and they'd just ended for the night. So they were taking time off of another job…for her? Wow. *Wow*. She almost wasn't sure what to do with that.

"Hartley, my dear, dear friend, you're missing the most important part of this news," Scarlett said.

"Which is?" she asked, grabbing her purse and pushing out of her car. The early October night was cool and refreshing.

"They're not having sex with anyone else!" Scarlett exclaimed.

"Because they're spending all their time working for me." She thought back over the week, and how many nights they'd stayed as late as—or even later than—tonight. Having squeezed her repair project in to what seemed like an already busy schedule, she knew they were juggling a lot.

"Because they're spending all their time *with* you."

"That's what I said," Hartley said, walking up the outdoor stairs to her third-floor apartment. The apartment itself wasn't all that special, but from her third-floor balcony, she had an amazing view of the sunrise over the water.

"No, you made it about the work. I'm telling you it's probably about you. The club's open until two in the morning, Hartley. They could come later, but Kenna says they're not. There are apparently a whole lotta disappointed submissives at Blasphemy." She chuckled.

Inside her living room, Hartley turned on a lamp and sat on the edge of the couch. Her mind reeled. Could Scarlett be right? Her belly went on a loop-the-loop at the thought that the men were interested enough in her that they'd stopped… doing whatever it was they did at Blasphemy.

She shrugged off her hoody, suddenly warm. What *did* they do at Blasphemy?

A sudden flash of half-formed, shadowy images rushed through her brain. Hands and mouths and bodies.

And it amplified the attraction she'd been feeling for them—both of them—by a factor of about a thousand. Because the week had been one long tease of being around their strong bodies, getting drawn in by their friendly banter and obvious expertise around boats, and seeing their toned abs when they'd use the hem of their shirt to wipe sweat from their faces in the cramped heat of the boat's cabin. Not to mention the way they looked at and flirted with her.

But what was she supposed to do about any of that? "Oh, God," she said, not really meaning to say it out loud.

"What?" Scarlett asked. "Oh, honey, I thought you'd like this news."

"I do. It's just…Scarlett, I don't know what I'm supposed to do with the fact that I'm maybe attracted to two men at the same time who are maybe attracted to me, too!" she exclaimed in a fast rush.

"Well…I think you just…go for it," she said.

On a groan, Hartley flopped against the back of the couch. "Sometimes, damnit…*sometimes* I just wish they'd make a move so that all I had to do was surrender to it. I don't want to make the decision or figure out what to do. I don't know how to just go for it, you know?"

A long pause, and then Scarlett's voice was gentle. "Hart, do you remember at lunch when you asked about how you'd know if you were submissive?"

"Yeah," she said, feeling like a limp noodle against the soft chenille.

"What you just said, *that* was something a submissive would feel. That desire to have someone else make the decisions and be in control, that wish to have someone else dictate what will happen and when and how. That's part of what it means to be submissive sexually. It doesn't mean that a person is weak or meek or lets others walk all over them. It's about wanting to yield control in the bedroom because that's what most gets them off."

Scarlett's words fell over Hartley like a waterfall, powerful and unavoidable. That…that was what she wanted. That was what she wanted with Jonathan and Cruz. God help her, she couldn't believe she was admitting that, even to herself.

But could she really let herself have it?

Hartley had walked through the door to A&R every one of the last eight days, though she hadn't yet walked through the door she suspected the men had been hinting at the day they'd just barely broached the three-legged elephant in the room. The door that led to…something with them. Her and the two of them.

An idea that still made her belly flip. And still aroused her. And still scared her, even after the epiphany she'd had during that phone call with Scarlett the night before last.

Yesterday when she'd worked with them, she'd allowed herself to really consider it. And it was clear from how turned on she'd been all damn day that it was an idea that became more and more tantalizing the more time she spent with them. Because she genuinely liked them. *Both* of them.

Jonathan's easy-going attitude, always so quick to laugh or offer a kind word. Cruz's intensity, an utter turn-on whether he applied it to the work on her boat, making her laugh, or even just looking at her. And her *like* wasn't of the *which of them do I like more?* variety. It seemed to her that they were a package deal—and her libido was interested in the whole package.

It was her brain she had to get on board. The brain that wanted to tell her it was crazy and reckless (and maybe even slutty) to want two men at once.

All of which was why she'd determined to stay focused on the thing that was keeping her up at night even more than her hormones—whether the repairs on the *Far 'n Away* would be done before the sailboat show. The sailboat show scheduled to start in just four days.

So as Hartley walked into A&R on Monday morning, shoulders knotted with tension, a stress headache threatening, she let out an audible little "aw" to find Jonathan and Cruz already working, despite the fact that their shop hadn't officially opened yet. These guys were totally going above and beyond, and it made her feel like she had someone on her side again after so very long of going it alone.

Well, two someones. Twice as special.

She climbed aboard the cat, made her way into the salon, and called out. "Hey, good morning. I brought breakfast." Hartley slid the cardboard tray of coffee cups and an accompanying pastry box filled to the brim with donuts, muffins, and croissants onto the table.

Cruz was the first to emerge from the companionway, wearing a form-fitting black T-shirt and a pair of jeans that hugged his hips and thighs like a glove. A glove she was maybe jealous of. Because, *damn*. "You're an angel, Hartley," he said, grabbing a cup of coffee with his initial on the side. "Good morning."

"An angel of mercy," Jonathan said, joining them with a big smile on his face. In a gray T-shirt and jeans, his jaw sported a sexy scruff and his dark blond hair was up in a messy knot on the back of his head the way he sometimes did when he wanted to keep his hair out of his face. She hadn't thought she loved man buns until she saw him wear one, but now she was a true convert! He popped the lid off his cup and froze. Then he sipped it.

"What? Did I do something wrong?" Jonathan took his with one cream and one sugar, while Cruz liked his with two creams and three Splenda. Or, at least, she thought that was right. This morning wasn't the first day she'd brought food with her, but today she'd taken the liberty of preparing the coffee for them. As hard as the men were working for her, she figured breakfast and a little TLC was the least she could do.

Cruz peaked under his lid, smiled, and put it right back on. "No, Hartley," he said, nailing her with a darkly pleased stare. "You're perfect."

Annnd there went her belly again, turning over as those butterflies did their thing for the millionth time.

Jonathan sipped his coffee again and nodded, his gray eyes glued to her. "Truer words…"

Was it warm in there? Or was it just her dying of need and a dash of embarrassment from the way they were devouring her with their gazes? Finally, she rolled her eyes. "I'm hardy perfect. And I'm not fishing for compliments, either. But no one's perfect."

Jonathan stepped closer, close enough that he could've reached out and touched her. And part of her, *God*, part of her wished he would, that he or Cruz would just start something, something that would sweep her away and suck her in. "Fair enough. But there *is* such a thing as being perfect for us."

Heat roared over Hartley. Her pulse quickened. Her nipples hardened. Her skin tingled. *Perfect for us.*

It wasn't the first time the men's flirting had gone a little further than was purely friendly. Nor did she think it hurt anything to flirt back, which she did, just a little, and just for fun. But it was the first time either of them had blatantly framed that around the idea of *us*. The first time they'd said it out loud, like it was normal.

Maybe it was? Maybe she was overthinking this whole thing?

He winked at her and smiled, letting her off the hook, at least for the moment. Though she had the distinct feeling that it was a temporary reprieve. "Grab a donut and come see," he said, nodding toward the passageway to the cabin.

"Who could resist an offer like that," she said, grasping a chocolate-frosted donut from the box.

Cruz gave her a wicked smile as he gestured for her to go first.

One that seemed to say, *Apparently* you *can resist our offer, Hartley*. Or maybe those were her own thoughts she was hearing. Because except for the fear that people didn't just go around sleeping with two men at once (did they?), more and more she found herself wondering why she was resisting this attraction to them.

Just go for it. Scarlett's words played on a loop in her head.

Stepping into the doorway to the cabin, Hartley gasped. "How late did you two work last night?" Her tone reflected the awe she felt. Because when she'd left, they'd gotten as far as installing the new platform bed and cabinetry, but none of the finishing woodwork that made it all appear one smooth, seamless piece. Now, that work was done. Along with the painting of the cabin wall where the hole had been.

Leaning against a cabinet, his arms crossed in a way that made the lean muscles of his biceps bulge, Jonathan gave her a look so sexy that it nearly stole her breath. "We worked as long as it took."

Damn if that didn't reach right into her chest. Because they'd done it for her. Again and again and again, they'd done so much for her.

"You must've been up all night. It looks fantastic," she said, her gaze darting around the space as she took it all in. "Almost like nothing ever happened. I'd never be able to tell if I didn't know what to look for."

"That was the idea," Cruz said, his sexy mouth sliding into a satisfied smile. "And the look on your face right now makes it all worthwhile."

She met his gaze, and her heart tripped a little. Because there was something that looked a lot like affection there. Affection and want. "You guys are amazing. Seriously."

"Well, we're not done yet," Jonathan said. "So eat up, because now we need to paint the bottom so you can have your baby back." He winked playfully. "Then she'll be shipshape again."

It was a big job yet to do, with just a few days left until the show. But she felt hopeful for the first time since this whole nightmare started. Hopeful…and not alone. "Then let's do it," she said.

Fueled by caffeine and sugar, the three of them worked side by side on the hull's exterior. Every so often, one or the other of the men had to step away to consult with one of their employees about the other projects they had underway. More proof of all that they were doing—and sacrificing—for her.

Nine o'clock came again, and she looked over her sailboat, gleaming bright with a second coat of paint. Now they just needed to apply sealant, and she'd be done.

"You guys did it," Hartley said, taking it all in. Then she turned to where they were standing, just behind her. "Thank you," she said, hugging Cruz first. "It's not enough, but thank you."

His arms came around her, warm and strong. "Of course it's enough, Hartley. You're welcome." He squeezed her tighter, tight enough that they were molded together from face to hips. And, Jesus, he felt good against her. All strong, hard muscles. She didn't want to let him go. But she did.

When she turned, Jonathan's gray eyes were blazing. And it set her body on fire as she approached him to show her gratitude. "Thank you," she whispered, peering up at him. Why did this embrace feel so much more weighted than the one she'd given Cruz? She put her arms around Jonathan's neck.

And he pulled her in like he was nearly desperate to hold her. "Damn, Hartley," he rasped. "You're welcome."

There was something in the grittiness of his tone, in the firmness of his grip, in the fact that the lateness of the hour meant that it was just the three of them in the workshop now, that set her body on fire. Suddenly, she trembled against him, arousal spiking her adrenaline.

"Ssh, we've got you," he said. *We.* Not *I.*

She unleashed an unbidden little moan and buried her face in his neck. He smelled of freshly cut wood, a hint of sweat, and something that was all masculine, all him.

Just go for it.

Hartley pressed a kiss to his throat.

"Fuck," he bit out. Against her lower belly, he hardened immediately, emboldening her as desire lanced through her veins.

So she kissed him again.

Jonathan pulled back until he could look her in the eye. And his were on fire. "Christ, Hartley, we want you. Both of us. Do you understand what I'm saying?"

Chapter 7

SOMEHOW, HARTLEY MANAGED TO PULL her gaze away from the intensity of Jonathan's, because something inside her disliked the idea that Cruz might be feeling left out of this moment. She looked at the other man, and found him standing stock still, as if he were restraining himself from moving.

As if he were restraining himself from joining them. And she hated that.

"Yes," she said, her voice a little shaky, the room threatening to spin around her. "I understand. I won't lie, it scares me, but I want you, too. Both of you." She aimed her last words right at Cruz.

He was at her side in an instant, his hand on her lower back, his shoulder touching Jonathan's. "No reason to be scared, Hartley. We only want to treat you good, to take care of you."

She looked from one man to the other. "But I don't know what…or how…" She shook her head. "I don't know if I'm…submissive."

Threading a hand into the hair at the nape of her neck, Cruz's voice dropped when he spoke. "Hartley, close your eyes and keep them closed."

She did. God help her, she did. Even though not being able to see what they might do to her made her tremble even harder. But that wasn't the only reaction her body had. Because she was suddenly wet between her legs.

"Open your mouth." That was Jonathan speaking now, a sterner, grittier tone to his voice, too. Swallowing hard, she dropped her jaw, ovaling her mouth. His cock hardener even more against her belly.

And then a finger traced the oval. Jesus, not knowing *whose* finger was an utter freaking turn on. Her hips jerked, and Jonathan's hold tightened around her back.

"Suck." Cruz, again. That finger slid onto her tongue, just a little, just enough for her to close her lips around. Was it Cruz invading her mouth? Or Cruz giving the command to suck Jonathan's finger? She wasn't sure which was sexier. And then the finger, wet with her saliva, slid in and out as she sucked.

When it finally pulled free, she felt bereft and couldn't restrain the whimper that spilled from her lips.

"Hartley, open your eyes," Jonathan said. It was a tone that was almost a growl.

She obeyed, and found them both staring at them her with such intense expressions that it made her knees go soft.

"God, you're fucking beautiful," Cruz bit out.

Jonathan gave a single nod. "*That*, Hartley. That was submission. The beautiful way you just gave into what we asked of you. That's what we enjoy. Commanding a woman to do things that will please all of us, that will make all of us feel good. Deciding how to give her pleasure, and asking for her willingness to receive that pleasure."

She unleashed a shaky breath, because his words seemed to lick over her skin. "I don't know the rules," she managed, her brain still holding her back, still holding onto one last strand of sanity.

Cruz crowded in closer. "Whatever you want to learn, we can teach you. But the rules don't matter right now. Except this one—say yes and you'll have our permission to come as often as you like tonight.

As her heart tripped into a sprint, Hartley knew she was done fighting her curiosity, her attraction, her desire. For them. So she surrendered, and it was as easy as uttering a single word. "Yes."

Yes.

The word hit Jonathan in a blast of heat. He threaded his hand into her hair, his fingers overlapping Cruz's where the other man had grasped her moments before. Linking the three of them in an irresistible connection.

Slowly, Jonathan lowered his face to Hartley's. His eyes locked with hers, burning darkly bright with need. And then his mouth claimed her mouth, soft at first, exploring. Then harder, deeper, until his tongue penetrated her sweetness and she moaned.

"Fuck, yeah," Cruz whispered, nuzzling Hartley's ear. Kissing and nibbling there.

Jonathan pulled away. "Taste her, Cruz."

"Oh, God," Hartley whispered, turning toward him of her own volition.

Cruz took her face in his big hands. And then he devoured her in a hungry, dominating kiss. And the picture of it had Jonathan aching hard, deep satisfaction flooding through his gut. This was right. This was so damn right.

Under Jonathan's touch, Hartley was trembling. No doubt a mix of nerves and adrenaline. Which just made him appreciate her bravery all the more—and her honesty in telling them she was scared. Jonathan was going to do everything he could to make sure she never regretted venturing down this path with them.

Because this was a path he wanted the three of them to walk

for a long damn time. He forced the thoughts away. Now was time to *feel*, not think.

When Cruz pulled back, Jonathan was right there again, kissing her, claiming her. Their three faces close together, their breaths coming harder, faster. But he needed more than this. They all did. So Jonathan walked her backwards, one slow step after another, until they were able to step up onto Hartley's catamaran.

"Are we christening my boat?" she asked a little shyly, but with a growing smile on her pretty face.

Jonathan chuckled and guided her into the salon. "You better believe it." He arched a brow and nodded toward the starboard companionway, the one on the opposite side from where they'd been working. "Aft cabin."

Standing in the space before another of the boat's three full-sized platform beds, Cruz took control. He came right up to her and grasped her by the hips. "This only goes as far as you want it to go. Something you may not know about a relationship between a submissive and her Dominant is that the submissive has ultimate control—all she has to do is say she's uncomfortable or doesn't want something to happen, and everything stops."

Jonathan nodded. "In BDSM, it's called a safe word. But all you have to say is stop or slow down, Hartley, and we will."

"Okay," she said. "And if...if I want it to keep going?"

Brave fucking girl. Jonathan grinned and winked. "Then we're all yours."

She gave a little laugh, and he loved the sound of it. To him, sex didn't have to be serious all the time. It could be playful and silly and even funny. "Well, I like the sound of that," she said.

"Good," Jonathan said, tugging at the hem of her shirt. "Then can I take this off?"

Hartley nodded, and soon the intensity returned between

them, as they all took turns kissing and removing clothes and touching, until he and Cruz wore only their jeans and Hartley was naked excerpt for a pair of navy satin underwear and a blue-and-purple watercolor heart tattoo on her chest—both of which contrasted beautifully with the pale porcelain of her skin.

"On the bed," Jonathan said, giving her a boost so that she sat on the waist-high edge of the platform. He and Cruz stood in front of her, side by side, shoulders touching. And that gave Jonathan a thrill, too, sharing this with another person, someone he'd cared about his entire adult life.

He'd always been able to find the human body sexy and appealing. Male, female—it didn't matter to him. And he was man enough to admit that Cruz Ramos was fucking hot. His muscles. The dark intensity of his eyes. The words that came out of his mouth, especially during sex, and how that revealed the inner workings of a brilliant mind. Yeah, all of that was damn attractive.

Jonathan had never acted on any of that, though, because Cruz had never given him any indication of wanting it. Hell, of even being open to it. But that was okay, because this was enough. Sharing a beautiful woman and knowing they were going to drive her wild. Together.

"Lay her out for us, Cruz."

The other man nodded and crawled up on the bed, kissing Hartley as he laid her back and climbed half atop her. Jonathan stretched out on the opposite side of her, until the three of them lay next to each other, the hardness of the men's bodies crowding Hartley's soft curves. They kissed for long minutes, and Jonathan knew they were both working to allow her to relax into the experience of being with two men. When Cruz claimed her mouth again, Jonathan moved his kisses to her throat, her shoulder, the slight mound of her breast. He sucked her nipple, and Hartley's back arched. She moaned into Cruz's kiss.

And then they traded. And Jonathan was the one swallowing her moans and sighs and gasps, while Cruz explored her body with his lips and tongue and hands.

Hartley's body trembled and writhed beneath them. "Oh, God," she rasped, brown eyes pleading. "I need more."

Cruz's gaze cut to Jonathan, and it was filled with satisfaction and resolve. Because that pleading beg was exactly what they'd been waiting for. An unspoken agreement passed between him and his friend, and then Jonathan kissed Hartley one more time. "We've got you."

He worked his mouth and hands down her body, drawing off the silky blue underwear as he moved. She was naked by the time he stood at the foot of the bed again.

"Spread your legs."

She did, without hesitation, fully revealing her arousal to him. Because her wetness was visible against the soft pink skin and neatly trimmed brown hair.

"I'm gonna enjoy you, Hartley," he said, kissing up her legs and leaning in. "And I want you to enjoy us right back." With that, his mouth came down on her, open and probing. His tongue licked, his lips sucked.

Hartley cried out, and Jonathan got even harder when her cry suddenly cut off. Peering up over her softly rounded belly, undulating from the way she writhed and thrust her hips against his mouth, he found Cruz kissing her again, his hand working over her breasts and nipples.

And that view…watching other people having sex while he was having sex…was a big part of why ménage aroused him so fundamentally. It added a dimension to the experience that he craved, and always had.

And it fueled him on as he ate her and licked her and sucked her until her arousal coated his tongue and she moaned non-stop. Drawing back, he brought his hand to her and slid his middle finger deep.

"Oh, yes. Oh, more," she said.

"Like this?" he asked, penetrating her with a second finger as he sucked her clit. He flicked it with his tongue while he fucked her with his fingers.

The sound that spilled from her was part moan, part whine. And it meant she was losing herself to this experience—and trusting them to treat her right. Raw masculine satisfaction raced through his veins at the thought.

"I want you guys," she whispered, her voice a high rasp. "Please."

"Come on my face and my fingers first, Hartley," Jonathan said.

"Jesus," she cried when he sucked at her harder.

Her hand fell on his hand and tangled in his hair as she pushed him down harder. He growled against her, fucking loving the initiative, the confidence to tell and show them what she needed.

"Give it to us, Hartley," Cruz said. "Then you can have our cocks."

The words had barely left his friend's mouth when Hartley was bucking and crying out, her pussy pulsing around his fingers. He sucked and fucked her through it, wanting every last drop of pleasure wrung out of her. Finally, she went limp beneath them.

But she wasn't passive, not in the least, because she reached out and grasped the waistband of Cruz's jeans. "I want all of you guys, too."

Grinning, Cruz worked off the denim, and Jonathan did, too. Before he dropped his jeans to the floor, he retrieved a condom from his wallet. And then he rolled it on as Hartley and Cruz watched.

Cruz stroked his own cock, thicker than Jonathan's but a little shorter. Jonathan tried not to stare, but he liked what he saw.

Cruz's brute strength next to Hartley's willing softness. "Slide off the bed, Hartley," Cruz said.

Jonathan helped her down and pulled her into his arms, glad that the size of the cat just barely allowed sufficient headroom for him to stand. He kissed her like they'd been apart, desperate and possessive. "Doing okay?" he whispered.

"So much better than okay," she replied. "And you…" She bit her lip, as if she reconsidered what she'd been about to say.

"Finish that sentence," he said, a hand tightening in her hair and forcing her head back, just a little.

Her throat worked around a swallow. "Was just going to say that you taste good with me on your skin."

Fuck. *Fuck*. This woman was so right for him—for them.

Suddenly, Cruz was right behind her, boxing her body in between both of theirs. And damn how Jonathan loved having both of them close. "Is that so, Hartley?"

She nodded and peered over her shoulder, meeting the other man's blazing gaze. "So good." And then she looked back and forth between them…as if, as if wondering if they'd kiss and see for themselves.

But Cruz took the moment in a different direction, closing the door it seemed like Hartley was playing with opening. "Then kiss him again," Cruz commanded. When she did, Cruz dropped to his knees behind her, and her moans told Jonathan where Cruz's mouth had gone.

And then, *Jesus Christ*, then Jonathan felt Cruz's hot breath against the head of his cock where it rested against Hartley's clit. It was everything he could do to resist thrusting it forward, and maybe score himself a tongue bathing, too.

Engaging in threesomes, it was nearly impossible to avoid touching both of your partners at some point, and Jonathan had always found those moments when he and Cruz touched each other to be erotic, even if they were unintentional. But just as he'd done now, Cruz always seemed to pull back from the edge of that line with him, so Jonathan didn't chance pushing the man somewhere he didn't want to go. Sometimes, Jonathan was sure he picked up on a vibe that seemed to indicate at least curiosity, if not full-on interest. But then the moment would pass—or get shut down, and Jonathan convinced himself that he'd misread his friend, or projected his own desires.

Hartley's fingertips dug into Jonathan's biceps as Cruz's explored her with his mouth. When he finally stood up, Cruz's lips glistened. "Fucking delicious," he said, licking her wetness off his mouth. "She's so ready for you, Jonathan."

"Are you?" Jonathan asking, wanting to hear her say it.

"Yes," she said. "For both of you." The sentiment hit Jonathan in the chest and made his cock jerk with need. And he wasn't the only one.

Because Cruz got back on the bed and braced his hands against the mattress, his cock jutting up between them. And then he said, "Bend over the bed, Hartley. Bend over and take me into your mouth."

Hartley felt almost drunk on lust and need as she did what Cruz told her, her upper body finding space between his muscular thighs. The warm brown skin stretched taut over his thick cock looked delicious, and she wasted no time bathing his length with her tongue.

The groan that spilled from his throat urged her on, made her braver, made her believe the guys could get as much out of this experience as she did. So she sucked him in deep.

"Time for both of us to fill her," Cruz gritted out, his hand falling on the back of her head, guiding, encouraging, but not forcing. Though she might not have minded that, either. Still, she appreciated that they were taking things slow, gentle, working her into a state that made it easy to surrender over and over again.

And, damn, it was so much easier than she thought.

Jonathan's fingers stroked against her pussy, gliding through the wetness there, and then that sensation was replaced by another—his cock at her entrance. Teasing, probing, then sliding deep.

She threw her head back on a moan.

"Fuck yeah, tell us how good that cock is," Cruz said, pulling her hair into a ponytail in one big fist.

"I…it's…oh, God…*good*," she babbled, the stretching and fullness foreign after going so long without sex. And that made it all the more intense.

"Christ, she's tight, Cruz. Just wait 'til you feel her," Jonathan gritted out. And, God, if Hartley thought hearing one man in bed was sexy, hearing the raw, lust-drenched utterances of *two* was even better. More than once, she'd gotten off from the *sound* of a porn movie alone. No visual required. And this was about a million times hotter. Because this wasn't fake. Being in the middle of it she could hear every little thing—rough exhalations, skin sliding against skin, the wetness of her mouth around Cruz at the same time that she could hear the wetness of her pussy welcoming Jonathan.

Then Cruz did force her head down, back onto his length.

"There it is," Cruz said, his tone almost like he was in pain. "Both of us inside you, Hartley. It's so damn good."

But Hartley barely had time to process the eroticism of his words before both men started moving. Jonathan's hips swinging against her ass, slowly at first, and then a little faster. And Cruz using the leverage of his arms against the bed to raise and lower his hips, fucking her mouth even as she sucked and moved her mouth over him.

It was, without question, the most erotic moment of her life, because it entirely turned her into sensation. No thoughts. No rights or wrongs. No reality beyond the one in which she found herself impaled by cock by two men who seemed as blown away by the experience as she was.

All Hartley could do was moan and suck and hold onto Cruz's hip as she braced herself against the impacts of Jonathan's thrusts.

And then Jonathan's hand came down against her ass. Hartley's mouth came off of Cruz's cock on a shout. "Again," she cried. "Please." There had *always* been something about being spanked—the sound of it and the pain of it and the slightly shameful heat of it—that drove her wild, and having it done to her in this moment shoved her toward another orgasm. Shoved her *hard*.

"Like that, do you?" Jonathan asked. "Tell me you like my hand against your ass while we fuck you."

"God, yes," she said. "Oh, please, yes."

When Cruz guided her mouth back to his length, Jonathan spanked her again. And again. And again. The orgasm was like a detonation, ferocious and total. She screamed around Cruz's cock, his hands holding her head down and forcing her to ride it out with both cocks buried inside her.

Cruz shouted out his own release. "Fuck, Hartley, take it baby." His cock grew in her mouth, and then his cum spilled against her tongue again and again until it was all she could do to drink it down.

"Jesus," Jonathan rasped. "You two are so hot. I can't—*Fuck*. Coming." One, two, three more strokes, and he buried himself to the hilt on a groan, his hands tight on her hips.

When Jonathan withdrew, Hartley went limp in Cruz's lap. She peered up at him, and found him looking down, an open expression on his handsome face that spoke of affection and satisfaction. Exactly what she felt, too.

And then Jonathan joined them, his chest pressed against Cruz's leg, his forehead close to Hartley's. "You took us so good, Hartley," he whispered, his hand on her hip.

"You took us perfectly," Cruz agreed.

"I loved it," she whispered.

"Good," Jonathan said. "Because tonight is just the beginning."

Chapter 8

THOSE WORDS RANG IN CRUZ'S ears, and it was as if his mind couldn't decide how to react to them. All at once, he felt satisfaction at what the three of them had just shared, because it'd been fantastic sex with two people he cared about. But fear also flooded through him, because Hartley was special. Her playfulness and sensuality and adventurous nature were going to steal Jonathan's heart. Whether his friend realized that yet or not, Cruz would've put money on it.

And where would that leave him?

The odd man out? An occasional fuck buddy as the two of them dated, then married and moved in together? Obviously, he was putting the cart about fifty-two miles in front of the horse, but that didn't keep his brain from doing it. Because losing Jonathan Allen was pretty much the worse thing Cruz could imagine happening.

But he couldn't claim him, either. Not the way he wanted to. Not when it would probably mean giving up his family. Fuck.

Before long, he realized that Hartley and Jonathan had fallen asleep against his lap. He pulled the pillows behind his head and shoved the seriously unhelpful thoughts away and let himself enjoy being at the center of their little threesome. With one hand, he played with a silky strand of Hartley's long brown hair, loving the softness of it, and the way the loose curls wrapped around his fingers. He let himself look at Jonathan, whose dark blond hair fanned against Cruz's ribs.

Nearly holding his breath, Cruz stroked his fingers over the blond. And a little more yet. Until Cruz's fingertips touched Jonathan's scalp as he threaded his fingers through the man's surprisingly soft hair. His stomach threatened to go on a free fall from taking this little liberty with the man who'd years ago stolen his heart. But he hadn't acted on it then either. Because before Cruz had worried about his family disapproving, he'd worried about what their brothers in arms would think.

Suddenly, Jonathan shifted, his eyes eking open as he peered up at Cruz. Cruz's heart nearly stopped. And then it *did* stop, because Jonathan smiled, pressed a kiss to the skin above his ribs, and then closed his eyes again.

And, Jesus, it was a good goddamn thing that the way Hartley was laying on him hid his dick, because Cruz was suddenly rock-fucking-hard all over again.

From a single kiss.

From a kiss from Jonathan.

Why did Jonathan kiss him? What the hell did it mean? Not once in all the time since their first threesome together more than a decade ago had Jonathan Allen ever kissed him.

Maybe the guy hadn't really been awake? Yeah, that totally could've been it.

Not that his cock was convinced, apparently. Because that fucker could've flown a flag in twenty-knot winds. Jesus.

And even if Jonathan's kiss had caused the erection, it was the view of both of these beautiful people sprawled all over him that kept him aroused. His love for Jonathan aside, had Cruz met Hartley on his own, he would've been interested for all the same reasons that Jonathan was. And even though his family could be a pain in the ass, the fact that she had *none* unleashed a protectiveness in Cruz's chest where Hartley was concerned. A protectiveness that made him want to hold her and take care of her and make sure she was never alone again.

So what if, in the end, they got together and he *did* become their fuck buddy? At least he would still be in both of their lives. At least he would still have some part of them.

Letting his head relax against the soft cushion of the pillows, Cruz closed his eyes and released a deep breath.

Some part would be better than no part at all, right?.

Yeah. Maybe he could live with that. Maybe he could see his way through to that being enough. Maybe.

Hartley woke up to the image of Jonathan's handsome face mere inches from her own. She smiled, because in the peace of sleep, he appeared younger, and she could almost imagine him at eighteen, tanned with sun-streaked hair, racing into the waves, a board under his arm.

But she didn't want the boy he'd been. She wanted the man he was now. She peered up over Cruz's ridged stomach at his ruggedly handsome face and the tribal black ink running down his upper arms. Yeah, she wanted the men that *both* of them were. Sailors, veterans, builders, friends. Men so confident in their sexuality that they could share a woman with another man.

At least, she wanted to *explore* this thing between them. It wasn't just that the sex had been amazing—which it had—it was that they'd made her feel so damn special. More than that, they'd made her feel a part of something bigger than herself. For the first time in so long.

And that feeling combined with being surrounded by all this sexy, hard flesh had arousal stirring in her blood again. It was like that dream she'd had, only better. Because this was *real*.

She shifted, and Jonathan's eyes blinked open. One side of his mouth lifted in a little smile. "Hey," he whispered.

"Hey," she whispered back. Mentally, she debated, and then she decided to follow Scarlett's advice once more. *Just go for it.* "Tell me…tell me to do something."

He arched a brow, heat chasing the lazy sleepiness from his gaze. "You need us again."

It wasn't a question, which made his words about a million times hotter. He understood what she was asking him. "Yes," she said.

"Suck Cruz's cock," he whispered.

The command made her pussy clench with need. Wanting to wake Cruz up with her mouth, not movement, she shifted as gingerly as she could. And then she took his cock into her mouth and tongued and sucked him until he grew against her tongue.

"Eyes on me," Jonathan said. She complied readily, hungrily. "That's it. Make him hard." His hand stroked the back of her hair, each stroke a little more firm than the last. As if to let her know that he could hold her down on that cock in her throat at any time.

Annnd that thought had her suddenly wet between her legs.

"Fuck," Cruz rasped, stirring beneath her. His hand fell against her head, too.

A moan spilled from her. She loved the feeling of both of them guiding her mouth.

"She likes our hands in her hair, Cruz," Jonathan said, eyes locked on hers. "Don't you?" She nodded as much as she could with her mouth full.

Now Cruz was the one groaning, and Hartley couldn't help but thrust her hips against the bed.

"God, I want to fuck her mouth, Jonathan."

"Would you like that, Hartley?" A fist in her hair, he urged her head up. "Tell me."

"Yes," she said, wound incredibly tight from just a few

moments of their dominance. "I would love that."

"Tell him to fuck your mouth." Jonathan's stare was dark fire.

Hartley directed the words to Cruz, whose expression looked almost pained with lust. "Please fuck my mouth, Cruz."

"Open," Cruz growled.

She did. And then Jonathan forced her back down on Cruz's cock. She ground her hips against the bed, desperate for friction, because being manhandled by the two of them was amazingly hot. And then it got hotter. Because as Cruz swung his hips upward, fucking her mouth in earnest, Jonathan pushed her head down onto Cruz's thick length, impaling her throat on his fat head. And all Hartley could do was take it.

It was almost enough to make her come. Instead, she moaned at the need twisting up inside her.

"She likes your cock, Cruz. And, Jesus, it looks good going in and out of her mouth."

"Fuck, Jay," Cruz rasped. At the edge of her consciousness, Hartley caught the nickname, but her brain couldn't concentrate on it, not when the two of them were so thoroughly and deliciously overwhelming her. "God, I'm gonna come."

"Yeah, Cruz. Do it. And then I'm going to taste it on her tongue."

Cruz came on a sudden, harsh shout, his release painting her tongue again and again. And then Jonathan was true to his word, because he grasped Hartley by the neck and hauled her to him so that he could devour her mouth in a brutally sweet kiss. His tongue invaded her so completely that for a second she couldn't breathe, but she was so turned on that part of her didn't care. Because it was incredibly hot that Jonathan didn't mind the taste of Cruz's cum, and it made her wonder what else Jonathan wouldn't mind…and whether Cruz felt the same.

With the combined tastes of Hartley and Cruz in his mouth, Jonathan wasn't sure if he'd ever been so turned on in his life. His tone was gritty as he bit out a command, "Cruz, sit up against the headboard. Hartley, I want a pillow under your ass and your back against his chest."

As they moved, Jonathan retrieved his last condom from his wallet. Laughter had him looking towards his lovers, and he found them in a near pillow fight as they shifted for him. Damn, but he hoped the smile he Cruz's face meant that the man was into this as much as Jonathan was. Because every new touch, new kiss, new way that they came together made him want it never to end.

He returned to the bed and got on his knees in front of them. "You two look so fucking good like that. Spread out for me." He rolled the condom on, his cock aching from want and his own touch. And then he crawled in closer, his knees under Hartley's thighs. Well, under Cruz's too, who had his knees drawn up to make a cradle for Hartley's body.

The two of them had done variations on the woman-in-the-middle position before of course, and it was one of Jonathan's favorites. Because it put him and Cruz face to face, eye to eye, so that they were connected by looks and breaths in addition to the woman they shared.

"Ready, Hartley? Ready for me to take you while Cruz holds you for me?" Jonathan asked.

"Yes, Jonathan. So ready," she said, and then she turned her head and brought her mouth to Cruz. "Are you, Cruz?"

Jesus, how hot was that? The way she made sure to include both of them in everything that happened between them? And it wasn't the first time she'd done it either.

And it was clear from the heat and affection flashing through Cruz's eyes that the other man realized it, too. "Take her, Jay. Make her feel as good as she just did for me."

"Yeah," Jonathan said, scooting closer until his cock was right at her entrance. He adjusted her hips to better receive him, and then he sank deep. Inch by mind-blowing inch until he'd buried himself to the hilt.

On a moan, her head arched back into Cruz's shoulder as Cruz looked down her body, his fingers going to her nipples. "Look how he's filling you," Cruz said.

Hartley's gaze lowered to where they were joined. "Oh, Jesus," she rasped.

"Tell me how good it feels, Hartley. How good does it feel to have our Jonathan inside you?"

Our Jonathan.

The phrase hit Jonathan like a blow torch, scorching him into his very soul. His gaze collided with his best friend's. For the first time, Jonathan allowed all the emotion he felt stay in his eyes. And he let Cruz see what he would.

Affection. Want. Need.

And, *fuck*, he was certain he saw each of those reflected back at him. At least, there was no question that was what Jonathan wanted to see anyway.

Hartley's words forced him back into the moment. "He makes me feel so full, Cruz. My pussy and my senses and… just everything," she said, turning her face into his again. "You both overwhelm me in the best way." She laced her fingers into Cruz's, and the gesture clearly moved the man judging by the passion with which he took Hartley's mouth in an aggressive kiss.

On slow ins and outs, Jonathan moved his hips, wanting to build this, wanting to make it last. He braced his hands on both of their knees, needing to touch them both, to hold them both, to make an unbroken circle of their lovemaking. It was so damn good, the way her pussy squeezed his cock, the lust-drenched expressions they both wore, the heat radiating off of both of their bodies, all of them rocking together as Jonathan moved.

He wanted more of that. He braced a hand against the wall over Cruz's shoulder, allowing his upper body to come down closer to theirs, and giving him more leverage to move harder, faster, deeper. His strokes thrust Harley into Cruz, who absorbed the impacts with his arms around her breasts and belly, their fingers still linked.

"I want you," Jonathan said. It was a statement of emotion, not physical need. And it was one he meant for both of them. So he didn't shy away from meeting Hartley's gaze as those words spilled from his lips. Nor did he refrain from looking Cruz in the eye and saying it again. "I want both of you."

Cruz's eyes were black fire, and Jonathan found himself wanting to push Cruz in a way he never had before. Wanting to see what, if anything, Cruz might be open for happening between them. Because, *God*, Jonathan would take scraps from this man if it meant that the three of them could have even more of this.

He kissed Hartley on a moan, one she fed right back to him as he picked up his pace. And then he eyed Cruz.

But when it came, the encouragement didn't come from himself. "Kiss him, too?" Hartley said softly, although it came out sounding a little like a question.

"Would you like that, Hartley?" Jonathan asked.

"If you would, yes," she said, her breasts bouncing as Jonathan moved.

Jonathan's stomach suddenly felt like it did whenever they'd gone on a do-or-die mission back in the navy. "Cruz?"

Hartley touched Cruz's face, silently encouraging him to turn to her. She kissed him once, twice, three times, her third one a playful lick that made Cruz growl. "Will you kiss our Jonathan?" she asked him.

One beat passed, and then another, until Jonathan was sure Cruz wouldn't let him do it. Jonathan scrambled for something to say that would deflate the tension suddenly ballooning around them.

And then Cruz grabbed Jonathan by the back of his neck and tugged him hard, pulling their faces together and making their mouths collide. The kiss was blistering. Harsh and consuming. Cruz's hand fisted in his hair, a bite of pain that made him see spots. Jonathan further hardened inside Hartley, his thrusts more urgent as Cruz's tongue plundered his mouth.

"God, yes, that's so hot," Hartley cried, her hand sliding between them until he could feel her working her fingers over her clit.

Jonathan moaned into the kiss, because he was going to lose it. From Cruz's surrender. From the tight heat of Hartley's pussy. From the fact that she was turned on by all of them being together. "Fuck, I'm gonna come," Jonathan rasped, his orgasm nailing him in the spine and driving him harder. Seeing both of their bodies move from the power of his thrusts made him feel like he was fucking both of them. And that thought was his doom. "I'm coming, I'm coming."

His whole body shook from the force of it, until he collapsed against Hartley's shoulder. He pressed a kiss there, his harsh breaths puffing against her skin.

"Hartley, baby," Cruz said, his voice deep with gravel. "The two of you made me hard again. I know we've put you through a lot tonight, but I'd fucking love to be inside you when I come."

Cruz couldn't think, couldn't debate, couldn't deny himself. He wasn't sure how he was ever going to come back from having tasted Jonathan's mouth, and right now, he didn't want to. Right now, he just needed to come from the goodness of it.

"Yes," Hartley said, smiling and kissing him softly. "All of us need to come together. That seems only fair."

"Sweet girl," he whispered against her lips. Sweet girl who somehow provided the bridge that'd made it possible for Jonathan to want to kiss him. And that unleashed an affection in Cruz's chest for Hartley Farren—an affection stronger than what he'd ever felt for anyone else.

Except Jonathan. And what he felt for his best friend just then made his heart feel too big for his chest. Now, Cruz had to wonder—was Jonathan bisexual, too? And, if so, why had they never crossed that line before.

You mean, besides your own fears and hang-ups, asshole?

Right.

It was a line of thought that required more brain cells than he currently had, especially when Jonathan withdrew from Hartley and removed his condom, his cock still half hard.

"Let me grab a new condom from my wallet," Cruz said, his hands smoothing down Hartley's belly.

"I got it," Jonathan said, reaching off the bed. He tossed Cruz the packet.

And then Cruz was ready. "Sit on my cock, Hartley. I want Jonathan to be able to see everything as you ride me."

Bracing her hands on his knees, she lifted herself so that she could sink down on his length. Cruz guided her with his hands on his hips, a groan spilling out of his as she slowly worked to take all of him.

"Oh, God, you're really big," she cried.

"Just go slow. You can take him," Jonathan said, kneeling beside them.

"Yes," Cruz said, gritting his teeth at the goodness of her slick pussy. When she was finally sitting fully on his cock, they both moaned. Cruz adjusted both of them so that he lay flatter and her legs were on the outside of his. "Lay back, baby. I got you."

She fell back against his chest, and he wrapped his arms around her.

And then he braced his heels against the bed and let his hips fly.

Hartley cried out. Her nails dug into his arms where they

held her. And her pussy squeezed him so goddamn tight.

"Fuck, Cruz is filling you so good," Jonathan said, his hand lazily stroking his cock as he watched them.

"Yes," she cried. "It's so intense like this."

"Make it more intense for her, Jay," Cruz said, nailing him with a lust-drunk stare. He wanted Jonathan to be a part of his first time with Hartley, too, just as Cruz had been for them. Hartley was right—all three of them *did* need to come together. If they had a shot at this thing. And Cruz wanted them to. God help him, he did. Because how often had sex involved this much emotion for him? For him, it never, ever had before. And it was because of these two people. These two people *together*.

Nodding, Jonathan came closer until he was leaning over where Cruz and Hartley were joined. Hartley bucked and cried out, and Cruz stared down her body just enough to witness his friend licking her clit.

"Yeah," Cruz gritted out, still fucking her with deep, steady strokes. "Want you to come again, Hartley. Want you to come on me. Damnit, I need to feel it."

But what he felt next nearly blew his mind. Jonathan's tongue against the base of Cruz's cock on every fast withdraw. They were just quick, teasing flicks, but each one hit him like a whip's impact, shocking and searing.

"I want to feel both of you come," Jonathan said, his face between their legs. Jay dove in to teasing them both with his tongue and his lips and his hands until both he and Hartley were moaning and thrusting and clutching each other tight.

"Oh, fuck," Hartley said. "I can't…it's too much…"

"Come, Hartley," Cruz said. "Come on my cock and Jonathan's mouth."

Jonathan focused all his efforts on her. It didn't take long. And then she was screaming both of their names and coming so hard that she shoved Cruz's cock out of her pussy, and the evidence of her orgasm ran down her ass to his groin.

"Yes," Cruz said, guiding himself back into her, the hold on his own restraint a fraying thread. "That was fucking beautiful."

And then he had no restraint at all, because Jonathan returned the attention of his mouth to tormenting Cruz. Flicking at his cock and his balls until Cruz was shouting and pulsing and losing himself in both of them.

When their bodies calmed, Cruz and Hartley went limp with satisfaction. And then Jonathan made their pile complete by stretching out with them, all of them touching so that Cruz couldn't tell who was touching him where.

And it was the best feeling of his life, this sense of belonging and completion.

What it meant in practical terms, he didn't yet know. But he wasn't ruining this moment by trying to figure it out.

Chapter 9

JONATHAN WOKE UP AGAIN BEFORE the sun rose, which was a good thing since their crew usually arrived around eight. He wanted to make sure Hartley got home safe before anyone knew where she'd spent the night. Not for his and Cruz's sake, but for hers.

"Hartley, darlin'. Wake up."

Her and Cruz's eyes opened at about the same time.

She smiled. "What time is it?"

"Almost six. I figured you wouldn't still want to be here when the guys arrived," Jonathan said, smoothing a hand down her arm.

Chuckling, she shook her head. "That probably wouldn't be the best idea."

Cruz rubbed the heels of his hands against his eyes. "We'll run you home, baby."

Damn, Jonathan loved hearing his friend call her that. Loved having just one more piece of evidence that they were all in this together. Especially after the lines that he and Cruz had crossed the night before. Lines that Jonathan hoped were obliterated for good.

"It's all right," she said. "My car's here."

Cruz grasped her chin in his fingers and brought their faces close. "Fine. But is it okay if we follow you to make sure you get home okay? We gotta head home for showers anyway." Jonathan appreciated the thoughtfulness of Cruz's idea, in part because it was evidence of the other man's affection for Hartley.

She smiled and nodded. "Of course."

They dressed and stripped the bed, making small talk about the day that felt totally normal. And then he and Cruz walked Hartley to her car.

"Jay and I rode together yesterday, so I can drive you if you like."

"Honestly, that would be great," Hartley said, digging in her purse for her keys. "Because my contacts are stuck to my eyeballs from sleeping with them in."

Cruz threw him a look asking if that was okay.

Jonathan nodded, hating to be parted from them. Which made him chuckle, because it was also good to feel that kind of longing for two people he cared for. "Fine by me."

It was a quick trip to her apartment, and then they walked her up. Hartley invited them into her little living room. "Want the nickel tour?" she asked.

Grinning, Jonathan nodded. "Of course."

"It's not much to look at," she said, leading them past the small galley kitchen, separated from the living room by only a breakfast bar, and into the single bedroom and bathroom. The space was neat, tidy, and decorated in blues and greens, like the sea they all loved so much. Finally, Hartley retraced her steps across the living room to the sliding glass doors. "But it does have this stunning view."

When they all stepped outside, it was clear what she meant, because the sun was about half way over the horizon, spilling golden light in an arc across the morning sky.

"It's beautiful," Cruz said, giving her a smile. "But nowhere close to the view I woke up to this morning." Then he directed that smile at Jonathan, too. And damn if those words and that expression didn't hit Jonathan straight in the chest.

He'd always loved Cruz. They were best friends and had been brothers in arms. But this…it felt like something else now. Something new. Something *strong*. Something that had gasped to life under Hartley's nurturing hands.

Her laughter was almost shy. "Well, yeah, that was pretty stunning, too."

The three of them stood shoulder to shoulder for a long moment, just taking in the beauty of the breaking day. It was a moment filled with such peace and satisfaction, as if everything was right in the world. And for just that space of seconds, it was.

Seeing her here in her own apartment, Jonathan was suddenly glad they'd met Hartley outside of Blasphemy. Because it had allowed their connection to Hartley to develop beyond considerations of sex, and outside of the rules of BDSM. Instead, their bonds had been built on a stronger—and hopefully more lasting—foundation of friendship, well-suited companionship, and shared interests.

Shared interests that obviously included sex. And the kind of sex Jonathan and Cruz craved at that. The kind Hartley clearly needed, too.

"You should sleep for a while," Jonathan said, brushing Hartley's golden brown hair over her shoulder. "Don't rush back to the workshop."

"What about you guys? You didn't get any more sleep than I did," she said.

"Four years at the Academy and eight in the navy taught us how to operate without it when we need to," Cruz said, giving her a wink. "Besides, we want to finish the sealant first thing this morning so that the *Far 'n Away* will be seaworthy by the time you need to set sail to Annapolis on Thursday morning."

"Then I'll see you later?" she asked.

"Stop by A&R whenever, of course," Jonathan said, regret slinking into his gut. "But Cruz and I are going to have to work at Blasphemy tonight and tomorrow night."

"Oh," she said, her dropping expression making it clear that she was doing the same calculations about their schedules that he'd already run. The ones that added up to them not being able to see each other again for more than a week.

Jonathan exchanged a look with Cruz, and then he gently turned Hartley so that her back was against the railing and she could see both of them. "Darlin', we need you to know. We're not going there to play with anyone else."

"That's right," Cruz said. "But we're part owners, and that means we need to take turns running things like the registration desk, security, the bar, and general monitoring of the floor."

She looked back and forth between them. "I understand. I know you've been taking off time for me. And it's only eight days until I'll be back from the sailboat show and Sailing University."

Eight days that felt like an eternity—and judging by her tone, Jonathan wasn't the only one who felt that way.

"Hartley, would you like to experience Blasphemy?" Cruz asked. "With us?"

Her grin was immediate, and it unleashed a raw masculine satisfaction in Jonathan's gut. "I think…yeah, I would. But Scarlett mentioned that there's a masquerade party coming up where people wear masks? I might like that for my first time there."

Smiling, Jonathan nodded. "It would be the perfect time. The public spaces will be tamer because there are a lot of non-regulars and prospective members who attend. But if you're feeling up to it, we can play in private, too."

She bit her lip, and it made Jonathan want to kiss her so he could bite it himself. "That sounds perfect. Except, what do I wear?"

"Don't you worry about a thing, baby. Go kick some ass in Annapolis. And we'll have something here for you when you return."

With that, they said their good-byes. Which involved fumbling kisses in her living room and at her door, until finally they had to go.

She leaned against the jamb, watching them walk away. And damn if the soft affection and drowsy satisfaction she wore on her pretty face didn't make leaving that much harder.

"Hey Hartley," Jonathan called from the top of the steps.

"Yeah?" She grinned.

"Remember that happiness we toasted to? The kind that made your father love being on the water?" Warm pressure filled Jonathan's chest at the admission he was about to make.

Her grin widened. "Of course."

"I think we might've found it."

Forty-five minutes later, they were showered, changed, and on their way back to A&R to finish Hartley's boat repair. And neither of them had brought up what had happened the night before. It was driving Cruz fucking crazy.

Finally, he couldn't take it anymore. "Pull over," he said, indicating a stretch of empty parking lot on the outskirts of the Marine Center two blocks from their shop.

Jonathan gave him a look, but did as he asked. He killed the engine to boot. Silence was loud between them for a long moment.

And then Cruz asked, "Are we gonna fucking talk about this?" just as Jonathan said, "So, about last night..."

Another moment of silence, and then they both chuckled.

"Fuck," Cruz said on a sigh.

"Yes, please?" Jonathan teased with a smirk.

"Shut up, asshole. Be serious." Cruz nailed him with a stare. Because he couldn't take teasing on this. Not yet. And not when his emotions were still so close to the skin after last night. And not when this mattered to him so much.

On a long sigh, Jonathan said, "Dude, what if I *am* being serious? What if I'm open? To anything, with you?"

"Since when?" Cruz bit out, defensiveness rushing through him as the ground shook beneath the foundation of everything he thought he'd known and everything he'd told himself he couldn't have. *What if I'm open to anything?* The words were a dream come true and a curse, because it meant that *anything* would come down to what Cruz was willing to do—not Jonathan, after all.

"Since…I don't know. A while. I mean, I've never been against the idea. Just, the more we've scened together, the more open I've become."

"But I've never known you to go after another man. Not in all the years we've known each other," Cruz said, reeling with each new word that spilled out of Jonathan's sexy mouth. The mouth that had kissed him. The mouth that he'd kissed. Damnit.

Jonathan shrugged, and the casualness with which he could discuss this should've been comforting. But Cruz couldn't take it that way, not when his head was spinning and his emotions were all over the place.

"What do I need another man for when you've always been there?" Jonathan said. As if it was as plain as saying that the grass was green.

"Jesus Christ," Cruz said, feeling like a caged animal within the confines of Jonathan's dark blue Jeep. He wasn't sure whether to flee or wrestle Jonathan over the back seat to find out just how open he really was. He sure as hell knew which options his cock preferred. Because this conversation was making him rock hard.

"Is this about Hartley, too, or just about you and me?" Jonathan asked, his tone more serious now.

"Mostly about you and me," Cruz said, gentling his own tone. "But, yeah, it's about her, too. Depending on what it is you want for the three of us."

"I want what the three of us had last night, in and out of bed," Jonathan said without hesitation. "The openness, the emotion, the connection—all of it. No more holds barred."

"But what if I can't do that, Jay? What if I can't do it for the long term?" Cruz asked, spilling part of his guts into the space between them.

Jonathan's gaze was direct, observing, evaluating. "I'd never push you into anything you didn't want, man."

"I know that."

"Then what are you really saying?"

Yes, what are you saying, Cruz?

He sighed. "You want to fuck me?"

One corner of Jonathan's mouth drew into a slow, sexy smile. "I would fuck the shit out of you my friend. In a heartbeat. And we'd both love every second of it."

Jesus fucking Christ. Cruz raked a hand through his hair and concentrated on not coming in his pants like a fourteen-year-old. "And if I wanted to fuck you? How would this even work between us, as Dominants?"

"It would work however we want it to work. Sometimes you in charge. Sometimes me. And for the record, don't think I haven't thought about you fucking me before, Cruz. Hell, I'm pretty sure I've jacked off to the idea once or twice."

Holy shit. "Then goddamnit, Jay, why haven't you ever said anything?" Cruz asked.

Jonathan arched an eyebrow and nailed him with a dark stare. "You know why. Hell, even right at this moment, I don't know whether you're bisexual and or you're gay and you've been faking your enjoyment of women all this time. Because you've had a wall built up between us on this whole topic—until last night, until Hartley helped take it down. You always back away any time I even approach crossing the line with you. And that was okay, really. I accepted it and appreciated what we did share. But now that I've seen over to the other side, I don't want that wall going back up."

Cruz mulled all of that, unable to refute a single word. Because it was true. But there was something he could say. "I'm bi. I've never faked a thing with a woman. I've just hid that I felt something more for you."

"Then I guess all of that's another thing we have in common," Jonathan said on a sigh. "Aren't we two assholes?"

Managing a little smile, Cruz nodded. "Apparently."

"So, does that mean you're not going to sit here and tell me you're not interested?"

"In you?"

"In me. In Hartley. The three of us together."

"Fuck, you know I'm interested." *But what if you love her more? But what if you get tired of a threesome after I've fallen in love with you both. But what if it hurts our friendship? But I'm also scared as shit.*

"But?"

Cruz shook his head, his brain and his ego not willing to let those words fly.

"You're worried about your family," Jonathan offered.

Looking out the window at the harbor, Cruz nodded. "Yeah, sure. It's either come out and lose them or hide and deny part of myself."

Jonathan's hand fell on Cruz's forearm, tugging his gaze back into the car. Back to the man trying to talk him into believing in a forever for which he never once dared to hope. "Buddy, you're already doing the latter. I know it's not exactly the same. But do they know you're a Dominant? Or that you're the part-owner of a BDSM club? Or that you have sex with multiple partners at the same time?"

The truth of that observation sank in. Sank in *deep*. So, yeah, hiding his bisexuality from his family ran along some of the same lines. "What's different is that, when we see them at the holidays, I'll have to deny who you and Hartley really are to me. And that'll fucking suck."

"It will," Jonathan said. "I won't deny that. But we can figure all of that out. And what we can't figure out, we'll fumble our way through. Either way, you'll have two people at your back ready to make it better."

"You make it sound so easy," Cruz said.

"Only because I want it so much," Jonathan said, the sincerity behind his words shining through in his gaze.

Jesus. Cruz wanted it, too. But his gut told him somehow, someone was going to end up hurt. And he didn't want that for any of them. Not for himself, not for the man he'd long loved, and not for the woman stirring new feelings in his chest, either.

It was the early morning of the second day of the sailboat show when Hartley found it. A little white box tied with red ribbon tucked into one of the outside zipper compartments of her suitcase. How in the world had that gotten there?

Standing in her hotel room wearing only a robe and a towel upon her wet head, she untied the ribbon and lifted the lid. And found three things inside. A note. A tube of lubricant. And a short, squat toy.

Hartley didn't have to be told where that toy went, either. And heat lanced through her as she unfolded the paper and found a man's scrawling handwriting.

Dear Hartley,
We're thinking of you every day, and we want you thinking of us,

too. Even more than that, we want you ready for us when you return. Ready for us in every way. So wear this at least an hour a day. And no coming. This time, you don't have permission.

See ya later, baby –
Cruz & Jonathan

"Argh!" Hartley cried, falling back on her bed, a huge smile on her face. Along with celebrating the relaunch of her boat yesterday and the bittersweet kisses they'd shared before she got underway, it was one more proof that they were thinking of her. After all they'd shared, she really appreciated hearing it as often as they wanted to say it. Because she was *way* out on a limb with these men and this relationship, something how much she missed them further confirmed. She was in this deep. Already.

Now this...this evil torment! And it *was* a torment when she had to go the whole day thinking about the butt plug waiting for her in her room. She'd had anal sex before with one boyfriend, but the guy hadn't been particularly adept at it. Hartley suspected that wasn't *not* going to be a problem with Jonathan and Cruz. She wasn't sure if that aroused her or scared her. Maybe a little of both.

Because they were clearly thinking of taking her every way they could. And maybe wanting to take her at the same time. Both of them. Inside her. Filling her until all she knew was them.

Jesus. It was either the hottest October afternoon known to womankind or she was having a lust-induced hot flash.

Finally, the second day of the show ended. Hartley closed up the *Far 'n Away* and bee-lined back to her room. And then she got completely undressed, opened the box, and uncapped the lube.

We want you ready for us...

She shivered, the promise of those words turning her on as

much as if the guys had been here with her.

Hartley started with lube on her finger that she applied to her rear hole. First slicking the outside, and then working some in, a little at a time. Until she'd been able to insert the first knuckle, and then the second. After a while, she got more lube and tried again, this time with two fingers. The stretching sensation burned, but it also felt…decadently good. Dirty and naughty and even kinda slutty. And that was hot.

Her arousal made her feel ready to try the plug, which she slicked with its own coating of lube. By no means was she an expert in anal plugs, but she guessed that this was relatively modest in size. Lord knew it was no match for Cruz Ramos, that was for damn sure. The comparison made her shiver. Because, holy shit. That man's cock was could have monuments built to it.

Laying back propped on one elbow, her knees drawn up, Hartley lined the plug up with the tight muscle of her rear hole. She gently pushed. And then pushed a little harder. Until finally, the muscle started to give way and the hard silicone eased inside her. It was a slow process to work the toy fully in. Suddenly, the widest part slipped inside, pulling a hiss from her throat at the intensity of the stretch.

And then it was done.

"Holy crap," she whispered to the empty room.

It was a different kind of fullness from having a cock or a toy in her pussy, but it was good in its own way. She got up to wash her hands and gasped. Because *walking* with a plug in her ass was its own riot of sensation. An unavoidable, shifting pressure. One that stimulated things inside her whether she wanted to be stimulated or not.

Clearly, the men she was falling for were pure evil. Or evil genius. Maybe both.

She cleaned up and donned a robe, and then she sprawled on her stomach and reached for her cell.

Knowing they were at Blasphemy, she entered both of their names into one message chain so she could text them both. *Received your gift. Making use of it right now. In related news: it's super HOT down here.*

Grinning, she hit *Send*.

And then she placed an order for room service. Just as she got off the hotel phone, her cell vibrated against the bed. She scooped it up and found a text from Jonathan.

Well, damn, now it's hot up here, too. Hope our gift fits just right.

Hartley's jaw dropped at his cheek, so she sent some cheek right back. *Not as good as your personal gifts will fit, but I'm making do.*

The three little dots indicating composition popped up immediately, making Hartley grin again in anticipation. *We'll give you ALL our gifts soon. That's a promise.*

Well, now you're just being mean because soon is still days from now, she texted.

The dots popped up. Disappeared. Popped up again. *Told you I was going to get my revenge,* he wrote back.

Laughing despite herself, Hartley's fingers flew. *I want my certificate back.*

Never, Jonathan replied.

Room service had just delivered when her phone vibrated again.

Cruz, this time. *Hi, sweet girl. What a cruel image you've put into my head.* He ended his message with a winky face.

Sorrynotsorry? I mean, that's what happens when you make me put a toy in my ass and tell me I can't come. She chose the sticking-a-tongue-out emoji to send back.

Aw, baby. I promise we'll make it up to you. Sorrynotsorry.

"Aaah!" she cried out, grinning like a loon in the privacy of her hotel room. Because her men were thoughtful and sexy and funny. And for the first time in a long time, she didn't feel alone, even though in that moment, she was.

Jonathan and Cruz had done that for her, and in the process, they were working their way into her heart. It was perhaps the craziest, stupidest, riskiest thing she'd ever done to that particular organ, but more and more she resolved to take a leap—and to hope they caught her. Both of them.

Because she wasn't sure she'd ever be this brave again if it didn't work out.

Chapter 10

THURSDAY NIGHT WAS THE FIRST night they'd been able to see each other after Hartley's work trips, which explained why they lay in a sweaty, sated pile in her bed. Smiling at the mess of covers they'd flung to the floor, Hartley wondered if she could ever bring herself to wash their smell from these sheets.

While she'd been gone, they'd texted constantly and had more than a few late-night phone calls that had allowed her to get to know them even better. Like, that Cruz had a million cousins but no brothers or sisters, and that he'd been to every continent and had some of the most amazing travel stories she'd ever heard, and that he could solve a Rubik's Cube in under five minutes—a thing which had earned him some fame among his shipmates, and not a little razzing, when they'd been in the navy.

Like, that Jonathan had been modest in describing his surfing, because he'd won the California state surfing championship his senior year of high school, and that his parents were total hippies who knew he co-owned a sex club and thought it was great, and that he couldn't sing on key but could play the hell out of a guitar and loved to sing anyway—much to Cruz's dismay.

Despite all of that, they'd obviously needed the physical reconnection, because the sex had been urgent and fast and breathtaking as the men took turns taking her. Laying on her side, Cruz would fill her pussy from behind, and then he'd pull out so Jonathan could fill her from the front. There'd been no talk of anal play, and the men had made her the center of it all. It'd made Hartley feel like she'd come home after a long, long time away. Longer even than just her trip.

"So much for the dinner I was supposed to make you guys," she said, smiling at the men where they lay on either side of her.

"Food's optional when the two of you are on the table," Jonathan said, amusement plain in his voice.

She laughed, loving his playful nature.

Cruz's low chuckle was more reserved. His intensity was one of the things she loved and craved about him, but sometimes he wore it like armor. Which she felt like he'd been doing since he'd walked through her door.

Worried, she turned into him and cupped his handsome face in her hand. "Hi," she whispered.

"Hi," he said.

Hartley kissed him, a soft press of skin on skin. "Are you okay?"

Something flashed behind those dark eyes, something that belied his answer. "Yeah."

She kissed Cruz again as Jonathan moved to spoon her, his head on her shoulder so he could be a part of this. It was right where she wanted him. "Whatever it is, you can tell me."

"You can tell *us*," Jonathan added.

Hartley nodded. "Please, Cruz?"

The expression on his face seemed full of shadows. "I love what we've found. The three of us." He paused like he needed to think about the words, to pick and choose them carefully.

"Hartley, you've given Jonathan and I things I never expected. The last few weeks, I've realized that some small part of me never truly believed it was possible to want two people—beyond sex—at the same time. But now I realized I was wrong. Because I want both of you. I *need* both of you."

Relief flooded through her, because she'd experienced so much of the very same journey. "I feel the same way, Cruz—"

"Wait," he said. "Please."

"What is it, man?" Jonathan said, his tone serious and concerned.

Cruz scrubbed a hand over his face. "I...I talked to my parents." He swallowed hard and pressed his fingers into his eyes.

"*What?* When?" Jonathan asked.

"Talked to them about what?" Hartley asked, pulling herself closer to Cruz and putting an arm around his waist, because he was radiating pain. And she honestly had zero idea how or why his parents would've put it there.

"I...I told them I'm bisexual." His swallow made a tortured sound. "And I told them I cared about Jonathan as more than a friend."

"Aw, Christ, Cruz," Jonathan said, reaching a hand between them to take Cruz's. "That was so fucking brave. What did they say?"

Hartley didn't need to hear the words to know. None of them did. But she wanted to be there for him, because she knew they weren't going to be good.

Cruz's voice caught. "They said... *Fuck*." He heaved a breath. "They said that I was going to hell. And that I wasn't their son anymore."

"Oh, my God, Cruz." Tears sprung to Hartley's eyes. "I'm so sorry, baby." She wrapped herself around him.

Jonathan scrambled over her to Cruz's back, putting him in the middle, and then he pulled the man against his chest. "That's such bullshit, Cruz. And I'm so fucking sorry. We'll be your family. And we'll pray they come to their goddamned senses and realize you're a man anyone would be proud to call their son."

Wetness hit Hartley's shoulder, and it made her tears fall, too. But they weren't all tears of sadness. Some of them were tears of anger. Because why would anyone throw away their family? As someone who'd lost hers, she would never, *ever* understand that.

"Jonathan's right. You are ours and we are yours. We choose you, Cruz. Do you hear me? We *choose* to love you. And we'll do it over and over again. Every day."

Emotion lodged a knot in Hartley's throat, along with a little self-consciousness. Because she'd just admitted something in the heat of the moment that she hadn't even fully admitted to herself. She didn't just care about Jonathan and Cruz, she was falling in love with them.

Cruz pulled back, his eyes glassy and wide. "What did you just say?"

Hartley didn't play coy. "That I…I'm falling in love with you." Heart hammering against her breast bone, she met Jonathan's gaze next. "With both of you."

"God, Hartley," Jonathan said, his voice thick with emotion. "Being apart from you all week, after everything we shared…I'm feeling the same way."

"Damn," Cruz said, rolling onto his back between them. Both Hartley and Jonathan braced a hand on his chest, and the closeness felt so intimate. "That's why I had to tell them, you know? I couldn't hide something that's becoming so important to me. I didn't want to hide from *anyone* anymore. The two of you and what we're building here is too important."

Overwhelmed by the power of all these revelations, Hartley kissed Cruz. Softly, deeply, putting into actions everything her heart was starting to feel. She pulled back, smiling at the change in his expression. Gone was the tortured man from moments before, and in his place was someone who looked like he'd just shed the weight of the world.

"I wish you'd told me about your parents," Jonathan said, leaning his face close to Cruz's. "I would've been there for you. You shouldn't have to carry that shit on your own."

"Kiss me, Jay," Cruz whispered. It started off soft, just as hers had, and then it quickly flashed hot, as if it were full of words they couldn't say any other way.

When they broke apart, both men were breathing hard, and Cruz nailed her with a stare. "I'm sorry, but I gotta ask. I gotta *hear* it from you, Hartley. Face to face. Would you really be okay if our lovemaking—" He gestured to the three of them, then grabbed Jonathan's hand and held it to his chest. "—included us being together, too?"

"Yes," she said, not even needing to think about it. Her head and her body and even her heart had known from the beginning that Jonathan and Cruz were a package deal. Now, the three of them were. It was only right that they all love each other. And as much as she'd worried over engaging in such an unconventional relationship, it was hard to care how others would view it when it felt so right. "As far as I'm concerned, we're together. In any way. In every way. All of us, equally."

"I told you she was perfect for us," Jonathan said, a little smile playing around his sexy mouth.

"You did." Cruz blew out a breath. "I'm sorry I even asked. It was just, after my parents—"

"You don't need to apologize," Hartley said, aching for him anew. But she had an idea she hoped might begin to heal the wounds his parents had caused. An idea for how he might start to move on. And she wanted to be the one giving them a gift this time. "But please, let me prove that I mean what I say. That I accept all of you. All of us. Make love to each other. Right here, in my bed. Right now."

Hartley's gesture reached down into Cruz's chest and branded her love onto his heart.

He'd already been falling for her because of how freely she laughed and her brave, adventurous spirit that allowed her not only to dive into this thing with him and Jonathan, but also to solo captain her catamaran all over the Atlantic—wanderlust was definitely something they had in common. Then there were the bittersweet stories of sailing adventures with her father, and the funny, endearing stories of homemade Halloween costumes she'd pleaded with him to make that she'd shared one night when they'd stayed up late talking on the phone. But even if he hadn't learned all that and more about her, the acceptance she'd given him alone would've ensured she would always own a piece of it. Her and Jonathan.

"Only if I can have my mouth on you, too," Cruz whispered to her, his pulse kicking up under his skin.

Her smile was so pretty as she tapped a finger against her lips. "Gee, let me think about that…" And damn if her playfulness didn't further light him up inside.

Jonathan's big hand cupped his cheek, turning Cruz's face until their gazes met. "What do you want?"

"You," Cruz said, simply. Plainly. For once, honestly. "I want you to fuck me while I eat out our girl. And I want you bare, nothing between us." Because Jonathan had been right—Cruz *had* built a wall between them. A wall of fear, and maybe even a little shame. And even if he hadn't overcome all the things that scared him, he wanted to be braver and stronger than that. He wanted to *try*. Because he had nothing left to lose, and only love to gain. And with Jonathan, Cruz knew he'd be safe. Not just because they got tested regularly as part of the club's protocol, but because it was *Jonathan*. And Cruz would never doubt that man would have his back.

Jonathan kissed him again, spiking Cruz's arousal. "I'm gonna make it so fucking good for you, Cruz."

Hardly able to believe this was about to happen, Cruz could only nod.

Then Jonathan peered at Hartley. "Darlin', where's that lube we gave you?"

She was off the bed in an instant, a sexy, naked streak as she moved across the room to where her suitcase still sat unpacked. "Here it is," she said, joining them again.

Shifting onto his stomach, Cruz patted the bed in front of him. "Put that sweet little ass right here, baby." Smiling, she did just as he asked, her legs spread wide on either side of his shoulders. Cruz planted a hand against her belly and pushed. "Lay back. I'm gonna want to get all the way in there." He winked.

Hartley bit her bottom lip, a thing that made Cruz want to growl. But then she leaned back against the pillows, opening herself to him fully. Just as he was doing for Jonathan, who straddled his thighs so that the long length of his hard cock rested against his ass.

A thrill of arousal lanced through Cruz. He'd played with a few submissives over the years who excelled at giving rim jobs and stimulating his prostate, though he'd never had a cock in his ass. But he needed Jonathan inside him too much to give into the nerves squeezing his gut.

Jonathan's lips were suddenly at Cruz's ear. "Make her come while I prep your ass."

The command made him thrust his hips into the bed, the movement tormenting him with too little friction to give him everything he needed. "Gladly," he said. And then Cruz filled the space between Hartley's spread thighs with his shoulders, his hands and his mouth going right to her already wet pussy. He sucked hard at her clit, and found her sweet and ready.

She cried out and her hands flew to his head, scrabbling

for purchase against his short hair. He *craved* her desperation. Wanted it to match the growing fervor of his own as Jonathan eased one slick finger into his ass.

Cruz moaned at the invasion. That it was Jonathan penetrating him made his cock swell and his balls ache. It drove Cruz harder, his tongue licking faster, more firmly, and one of his fingers slid into her pussy.

And then Jonathan added a second finger to his ass and moved them in a gentle in and out that made Cruz need more. And it also gave him an idea. He withdrew his hand from Hartley, wringing a whine out of her that made him smile. Then he reached back to Jonathan. "Coat my fingers good, Jay. I'm gonna work Hartley's ass, too."

"Good fucking idea," Jonathan bit out, his voice full of dark arousal.

Cruz peered over his shoulder to find his best friend's expression an absolute mask of raw desire, and it was fucking hot.

When his fingers were slick, Cruz arched a brow at Hartley. "You ready for a taste of what the three of us are going to do together someday soon?"

"Yes," she whispered, her voice a raw scrape. "Show me."

Holding her ass cheeks apart with one hand, he eased the middle finger of his other into her tightest hole. And when she seemed good with that, he slid his pointer finger into her pussy, too. Hartley cried out at the double penetration and wriggled her hips, and he sympathized with her torment, because just then, Jonathan slipped a third finger into Cruz's ass.

"*Fuuuck*," Cruz rasped, putting his mouth back to work on Hartley's sweet pussy to distract himself from the stretching burn. He licked her and sucked her and nibbled at her, and all the while his fingers fucked her in a shallow in and out.

"I need in you now, Cruz. Jesus, I need it," Jonathan rasped, penetrating him faster with that thick trio of fingers.

"Do it," Cruz said, going at Hartley harder, needing her cum on his fingers and tongue. And then she gave it to him in a glorious clench of muscles, her whole body bowing.

"Cruz, God, coming!" she cried out, her pussy and ass pulsing around his fingers as her whole body writhed.

Before it was even over, Jonathan spread Cruz's cheeks with one strong hand and lined his cock up with Cruz's ass. And then slowly, so maddeningly slowly, he was taking the only thing Cruz had never given to another person.

The intensity of the sensation pulled a gut-deep groan out of him. "Aw, *Christ*, Jay."

Jonathan smoothed his hand up Cruz's back. "My cock looks fucking good sinking into your ass. And it feels even better."

"You guys are so hot together," Hartley said, lacing her fingers with Cruz's free hand. Because he hadn't withdrawn his fingers from her.

"Jesus," Cruz moaned, unable to control the words spilling from his mouth. Because it hurt like hell, but the pain was like a fire that cleansed him of all the lies he'd told himself, all the masks he'd hidden behind. "Jesus, shit, *Jesus*. So fucking intense."

But Cruz didn't know the half of it, because just then, Jonathan withdrew almost to his tip before driving back in again. The stroke wrung a shout out of Cruz and had him involuntarily thrusting his cock against the bed.

"Another inch and you'll have all of me," Jonathan rasped. "You ready?"

"Shit, no," Cruz bit out, half a chuckle in his tone.

"Yeah, you are," Jonathan said. "We both are." As he spoke, he bore down, *down* until every muscle in Cruz's body braced against the impact of Jonathan bottoming out deep inside him. "There it fucking is."

The grit in his lover's tone eased the burn inside Cruz—only to give rise to a whole other burn, the searing heat of need. "Move in me. Christ, I need you to move."

With that, Jonathan did. Slower at first, and then setting a steady rhythm that had him pulling almost all the way before plunging deep.

Right in front of him, Hartley's fingers circled over her clit. And the fact that she was getting off on him and Jonathan fucking directed the pain in a whole other direction. One full of dark, decadent pleasure. "Tell me how our Jonathan's cock feels, Cruz," she said, using his own words against him.

"It feels like every place inside me is finally full," he said, the words spilling out of him unfiltered, unedited, unvarnished.

"God, that's how you both make me feel," she said, her fingers moving faster.

"And we're gonna keep making each other feel that way," Jonathan said, his weight coming down on Cruz's back. His words were a promise, a vow, an oath that, in that moment, each one of them took. Their faces close, Jonathan claimed Cruz's mouth in a breath-stealing kiss. "Now put both of your fingers in Hartley's ass while I fuck yours."

Drawing up her knees, Hartley opened herself to them even more. "Do it," she whispered.

But he needed a moment to react, because Jonathan started fucking him in earnest again. The change in position had the man's long cock stroking his prostate over and over until all could do was rut against the mattress beneath him, jacking himself off as best he could while another man fucked his asshole.

Finally, Cruz gritted his teeth against the lust flooding through him and moved both of his fingers to Hartley's slick rosebud. Slowly, so damn slowly, he sank deep. "Make yourself come while I finger-fuck your ass," he growled, his voice wrecked from the storm of emotion and need they'd unleashed inside him.

"Not gonna take long," she said, her fingers alternating between sinking into her pussy and swirling the slickness she found there against her clit.

"How about for you, Cruz? You gonna come while I fuck you?" Jonathan said, his voice like gravel as he reached one hand under Cruz's stomach and fisted his cock.

And, Jesus, the touch combined with the raw desire in the other man's voice was like pouring gasoline on a fire. It shoved him toward what was going to be a monster release. Shoved him *hard*. "Yes."

Jonathan banded his other arm around his shoulder and throat. "Then fucking come. Because I'm about to give you everything I've got." His hips flew then, a relentless, punishing, amazing fury of movement that drove Cruz's cock into Jonathan's hand in a hard, undeniable rhythm.

"Cruz, come. Please come. Because I'm coming, too," Hartley said, her ass tightening around his plunging fingers. "Oh, God, I'm coming *now*."

Sensation spiraled through Cruz's body until he *had* to thrust against Jonathan's tight grip, his back bowing, his muscles going rigid. And then his release exploded out of him against his own stomach and a yell ripped out of his throat.

"*Cruz!*" Jonathan rasped, his strokes suddenly choppy and fast. "God, Cruz. Fucking take all of me." The words were a shout in his ear as Jonathan strained and then froze above him, his cock pulsing in his ass, his release filling him up and spilling over.

Unable to hold his head up, he went limp in the circle of Jonathan's strong arm. He had just enough presence of mind left to ease his fingers free of Hartley and clasp both of her hands in both of his.

Cruz was a sweaty, messy, sticky, sore mess.

And it was the best he'd felt in his whole damn life.

With the two people who accepted him most in the world. With the two people who totally, completely, and irrevocably owned his loyalty and his heart.

Jonathan stepped out of the shower and wrapped a towel around his waist. He felt drunk with satisfaction, especially when Cruz and Hartley stepped out after him, laughing and debating whether to order Chinese or pizza. Hartley's apartment was nearly a shoebox, but it did have two things going for it—that incredible view off the balcony, and a big shower stall they all could share.

But a big part of him wanted to relocate them to his apartment, if only because he had a king-size bed—a bed he really badly wanted to see the two people he loved lying and sleeping and fucking on. Though he certainly wouldn't have minded the music of Hartley's laughter filling his space or living with her habit of excitedly sharing quotes from things she'd read that moved or inspired her, nor would he have minded having Cruz's amazing black-and-white travel photos covering his walls or having his freezer filled with the evidence of the man's ice cream addiction. And no way would Jonathan say no to coming home to both of them at the end of the day.

There was, for him, no denying that *love* was exactly what he felt.

Not after Hartley's big heart had found the perfect way to take care of Cruz in the aftermath of his terrible revelation. Not after her selfless gesture and open-mindedness had brought them all closer than ever before. And not after Cruz had finally surrendered to this thing that had been building between the three of them—and in the process gave Jonathan one of the most intimate experience of his life.

In a way, they reminded him of the old, abandoned church he and his partners had renovated for the club that became Blasphemy. That great vaulted ceiling only stayed up because the buttresses worked together to distribute the weight and support the structure. And every buttress was needed to keep the whole thing standing. It seemed to Jonathan that he, Cruz, and Hartley were the same way. Each of them requiring the other two to get everything they needed. Each of them helping hold the other two up.

"How about it, buddy?" Cruz was asking. "Pizza or Chinese?"

Jonathan smirked. "Is there a reason we have to choose?"

Cruz rolled his eyes. But affection was plain on the man's face. And Jonathan intended to keep it there if it was the last thing he did. "Fine. I'll order."

Brushing her wet hair in front of the mirror, a towel tucked around her chest, Hartley called out. "Get breadsticks, too."

"Got it," Cruz said from the other room.

Jonathan wrapped his arms around Hartley from behind. "Thank you for the way you took care of him."

She shook her head, a small, sweet smile on her face. "That's what we do."

"Yes, it is," Jonathan said. The sentiment hitting him with its rightness, hitting him down deep. "You are the center of us, Hartley. I hope you know that."

She turned in his arms and laced hers around his neck. "We're all at the center at one time or another. *You* were the one who brought Cruz and I together at the start, remember?"

"How were we so lucky to find you?" he asked, leaning down for a slow, soft kiss.

A few minutes later, they were all dressed again. And while Hartley threw the sheets in the washing machine, Cruz grabbed a gift out of his car and placed it on the breakfast bar.

She returned to the room and froze, a grin settling onto her face. "What's that?"

"Baby," Cruz said, giving her a look. "There's only one way to find out."

"You guys are going to spoil me with all these presents," she said, eagerly ripping off the floral paper.

"That's the plan," Jonathan said, chuckling at her enthusiasm.

He and Cruz stepped closer. They'd spent a lot of time over the weekend picking this out.

She tore open the box and gasped. "This is *beautiful*." She lifted out a traditional full-face mask—a black-and-blue carnival number with a fan of feathers to hide the edges of the face, too. "But wait, there are two," she said, picking up a second one made of a stick-on lace that would cover the top half of her face and looked almost like a tattoo when applied.

"We wanted you to be able to choose how much of your face was covered," Cruz said.

"Wow. These are both so cool," Hartley said, setting them aside to pull out the black gown beneath. "Oh, my God." She held the floor-length and *very* sheer lace-and-chiffon number in front of her. It had a severely plunging V-neckline, a bodice made of lace cutouts that appeared to float over the skin, and a hip-high slit up one leg that Jonathan was dying to see on her. "This is the most gorgeous thing I've ever owned. Thank you so much." She hugged it to her.

"Told you we'd take care of you," Cruz said.

She went right to him and threw her arms around his neck. "It's amazing. *You two* are amazing." She hugged Jonathan next.

He grinned, thrilled that she liked what they'd chosen for her. "The masquerade party's going to be a great night. We have an old friend coming into town we're looking forward to introducing you to." Leo Sinclair was a buddy from the navy, a man who moved around a lot and therefore they hadn't seen him in a long while. He'd called a few days before to say he was passing through on his way out to Vegas, and they'd harangued him to come to the party despite his insistence that it wasn't his kind of thing. That might've been true to a point—but they knew well enough that he was a Dominant, too. So they'd twisted his arm, because none of them were sure when they'd get another chance to visit.

"I can't wait to meet more of your friends," she said, spinning with the dress to see how the chiffon skirt flowed. Her delight made him want to give her a present every day. Hartley Farren was one of those people who found joy in small things, and he really appreciated that about her. "I just hope I don't embarrass you guys."

"You never could," Cruz said, pulling her into his arms. "We'll teach you the basics, and the rest will come in time."

"Absolutely," Jonathan said. "We can talk over dinner and tell you everything you need to know. Show you a few things, too." He winked, loving the color that rose on her cheeks.

"Okay, you know I'm all in," she said. "And I'm dying to see exactly what Blasphemy is all about."

Chapter 11

DRESSED IN A GOWN THAT made her feel like a princess—even if a somewhat risqué princess, what with all the skin that showed through the lace cut-outs and see-through chiffon skirt—Hartley stepped onto the main floor at Blasphemy and was immediately in awe.

The space was huge. Music echoed against the soaring ceiling, the colorful frescoes on the walls, and the massive stained-glass windows that hung along the whole length of the room. Thick marble columns lined the open area and a huge round bar dominated the center of the space.

"Welcome to Blasphemy," Jonathan said, a proud smile on his face—at least, on the part of his face she could see. Because he wore a cool black leather wolf mask, tooled and engraved with a painted design, and he'd left the past two days' worth of scruff on his jaw to complete the look. Shirtless, he wore only black boots and a pair of jeans that made his ass look freaking hot.

"This is amazing! You guys helped do all this?" Hartley asked, still trying to take it all in as they moved further into the room, through a crowd of people wearing masks and costumes as colorful and varied as the stained glass above them.

"Yeah," Cruz said from beneath a carved white Phantom

mask. He wore a bowtie around his throat and black dress pants and shoes. Together with those striking tribal tattoos on his arms, his costume was sexy as hell. "All of us played a part in saving and renovating the building. And now it's our second home." He winked and brought her hand to his mouth to kiss her knuckles.

And that had her gaze focusing on two things she'd never seen until tonight. The first was a black leather cuff Cruz wore knotted around his wrist. Jonathan, too. It bore a Gothic letter *M* that stood for Master, and it was one of the most erotic things she'd ever seen in her life. It took her attraction for them to a whole other level, especially as she witnessed people showing them both such deference and respect—the deference and respect due to the club's twelve Master Dominants. It was a heady thing to see. And the second new sight was the red leather cuff *she* wore around her own wrist—red for *attached submissive*.

Once, she hadn't been sure what she thought of that label. Now Hartley knew it meant she was theirs. And they were hers. And that she wanted to please them every way she could. She couldn't find one thing wrong with any of that, especially after what they'd shared at her apartment two nights before. Her chest still ballooned with a warm pressure every time she thought about all the ways they'd come together.

"You like the way these look, don't you?" Cruz asked, eyeing her through his mask.

"Yes, Sir," she said a little shyly, because the *Sir* still felt new and different spilling from her tongue. But she couldn't deny that saying it turned her on, especially when their expressions reacted to hearing it. Reacted with *lust*. It was just one of the things they'd taught her during their conversation over a buffet of Chinese and pizza. A training lesson that had led them right back to her bed...

When they reached the bar, they ran almost immediately into

two people Hartley recognized despite their masks—Scarlett, whose long hair gave her away, and Cassia, whose lace mask was so sheer that it was mostly decorative. The lace one Hartley wore was nowhere near as sheer, but its design, almost like a tattoo of black jewels dripping down her face from forehead to cheeks, made her feel so sexy that she'd chosen it over the one that offered more coverage.

"Hey!" Scarlett was the first to notice her. "Oh, my God, you're really here!" And then she schooled her expression. "Hello, Master Jonathan, Master Cruz."

Her guys smiled and greeted the women. Then Jonathan—or Master Jonathan, Hartley needed to get used to that, too—turned to her. "Hartley, would you mind if I talk to Scarlett for a second?"

"Of course not. *Sir*," she rushed to add, curious but quickly swept into conversation with Cass. "Where's Kenna tonight? Is she here?"

"She and Master Griffin are doing a bondage demonstration. Up on the stage." Cassia pointed to the far end of the room, and Hartley was immediately intrigued. She wasn't sure if bondage could be her thing, but then again, she hadn't been sure that two men could be her thing either. So her default, from now on, was to try *everything*. So far, that hadn't steered her wrong where her men—her *Masters*—were concerned, had it?

"I hope I can catch some of that." She leaned in closer. "Now, tell me, where's your Dom?"

Cassia's grin was immediate—and blindingly happy. "Master Quinton. The crazy, hot, funny one behind the bar."

Smiling at the description, Hartley turned and pressed onto tiptoes. Through the crowd, she caught a glimpse of the man in question—he wore a white cowboy hat and a black Lone Ranger mask, and had an expressive face and a swagger about the way he moved. "Very nice, Cassia. Hi-ho, Silver." She waggled her eyebrows.

"Oh, not you, too," she said, exasperated. "Master Quinton has been saying that all night." She gestured to her dress. Her *silver* dress. "Why do you think he put me in this?"

Hartley laughed, liking Master Quinton already and she hadn't even talked to him yet. "Someone's Dom obviously has a good sense of humor. Still, you look gorgeous in it."

Cass smiled. "Well, thank you."

Her men returned with Scarlett, who had an about-to-burst grin on her face.

"Baby," Master Cruz said, leaning in to Hartley's side. "Please wait for us. We're going to find our friend, Leo. He's here somewhere. We'll be right back."

"Okay, sure," Hartley said.

Master Jonathan kissed her cheek. "Thanks, darlin'. Sure you'll be okay?"

"Absolutely, Master Jonathan." She grinned when his eyes narrowed at hearing her say the title. Hartley had already agreed to play privately with them in one of the themed rooms, but if she hadn't, that look might've been enough to convince her. When they disappeared into the crowd, she turned back to her friend. "What was that about?"

Scarlett's expression looked like she was about to burst. "They asked if they could introduce me to someone. And now I'm freaking out." She laughed, and her happiness—nervous though it was—made Hartley happy, too. And feel even more affection for the men making her friend feel this way. Though she was going to have a talk with them—because next time she wanted to be in on the matchmaking.

"Don't freak out," Cass said. "Masters Jonathan and Cruz wouldn't hook you up with anyone they weren't absolutely sure about. And you don't have to do anything you don't want to do."

"I know," Scarlett said, blowing out a breath. "I know. I got this."

"You totally do," Hartley said, excited for her. "Hey, do you think it would okay to move around the bar a little so we could get a peek at the stage? A bondage demonstration might make a really good distraction."

They hadn't moved ten feet when Hartley's Masters emerged through the crowd, a dark-haired man in a plain black mask at their side.

She turned to Scarlett. "Oh, that must be their friend."

Under her sparkling black-and-red cut-out mask, Scarlett's eyes went wide. And she wasn't the only one who liked what she saw judging by the stunned expression on the man's face. And it made Hartley want to squee to see someone react to her friend the way she deserved—with awe, with desire, with respect.

Master Jonathan was smiling as he made introductions. "Leo, this is Hartley Farren, and her friend Scarlett Rose. Ladies, you may address Leo as *Sir* since he is not a Blasphemy Master."

Nervous at the possibility of making a mistake, Hartley gave him a smile and a nod that Leo returned. But he really only had eyes for Scarlett, who stood stock in her skimpy red satin slip still waiting to follow the man's lead. Watching them—and feeling the instant chemistry radiating off of them—made Hartley bite her lip to hold back the grin that threatened at the apparently very good match her men had made. Cruz winked at her, and heat filled her cheeks.

Finally, it was Scarlett who broke the tension between them. "It's nice to meet you, Sir."

Leo's eyes flashed through his mask. "The pleasure's mine. I hear we're both new to Blasphemy."

"Yes, Sir," Scarlett said, her eyes still on him.

"Scarlett helped convince me to give it a try," Hartley said. "Now I'm just hoping I don't mess anything up."

Master Jonathan took her hand. "You're not doubting that we'll guide you every step of the way, are you?"

"Oh, no. I mean, no, Sir," she said.

"Maybe we need to show her exactly what that means," Master Cruz said, his voice full of dark, sensual promise—a promise that shot heat through her blood.

Master Jonathan nodded and tugged Hartley between them. "Mmm, maybe we do."

Even as Leo continued to study Scarlett, Hartley couldn't help but be aware that they were watching her interaction with her Doms, too. And it was intriguing having others observe them, wonder about them, *know* that they were together. A threesome.

"Come with us, little one," Master Cruz commanded. "It's time for your first lesson."

"Lesson?" Hartley asked, her belly going on a loop-the-loop.

Master Jonathan flanked her other side, guiding them away. Hartley wanted to tell Scarlett to have a good time, or good luck, or even *just go for it!* But then Jonathan said, "No speaking unless asked a direct question. Leo, Scarlett, I'll check in with you later. Have fun."

Nervous energy rattled through Hartley as her men took her by the hands and led her deeper into the club. What did they have planned for her?

She both wanted to know and wanted to be surprised, and that was another thing she was learning about their world of domination and submission—there was so much pleasure to be had in *not* knowing, in not being in control, in not having to decide. Everything leading up to this moment had been one long session of foreplay, and Hartley was suddenly ready to find out exactly what they wanted her to learn about the world of BDSM, about the world of Blasphemy.

As they cleared the bar, the stage came into view. It dominated the whole end of the room, located where the church's altar must've once been. But even more attention-grabbing were the two people currently on that stage—a big, muscular black-haired man with tattoos all over his body, and a gorgeous yellow-haired woman currently suspended from the ceiling in a complicated and beautiful arrangement of ropes. Kenna. It was Kenna bound that way. Kenna being treated to a fast series of smacks from the flogger Master Griffin wielded. Kenna who was moaning when those smacks fell against her ass and breasts, and between her legs.

Hartley gasped, then pressed her fingers over her mouth.

"It's okay, baby," Cruz said, pulling her in against his chest. "We can watch for a minute. I think you see something you like."

And she did. Because they were beautiful together. Beyond the artistry of the ropework, there was an obvious chemistry between them—and an intensity that made it feel like they were the only two people in the room. Arousal stirred in Hartley's blood as she wondered if she, Jonathan, and Cruz looked that way when they were together.

She shifted her thighs together, the sensual display getting her hotter by the minute.

"Master Cruz," Jonathan said. "I think our girl needs us."

Cruz nipped at her ear, and his voice was nearly a growl there. "Mmm, I think you're right. Let's go."

They led her out the side of the space, but before they got very far, two men waved them down. Two seriously intimidating-looking men. The first man wore a sharp, black-on-black suit and had dark hair and even darker eyes, piercing as they peered at her through a mask that covered half his face, making it appearing that he was half flesh, half carved, black skull. Beside him, the other man was shirtless, but tattoos covered most of his chest and arms like an armor of ink. It was a fitting analogy given the simple, hard metal eye mask he wore over a harsh, masculine face.

The men shook hands, clearly friends. And the handshakes made her realize that both wore the wristbands of Blasphemy

Master Doms, meaning their were Jonathan and Cruz's business partners, too.

"It's damn good to see you, Master Hale," Cruz said. "Been too long."

The man crossed his arms, making the designs on his skin move with his muscles. "Business travel. You know how it is. Good to be back, though."

"Hartley," Master Jonathan said. "I'd like to introduce you to Master Alex."

The man in the suit gave her a nod. "Hello, Hartley." Despite his politeness, there was something about him that made her want to take one step back. She couldn't explain it.

"Hello, Sir," she said.

"And this is Master Hale," Jonathan said. "This is the man responsible for bringing us all together to found Blasphemy."

She smiled. "Hello, Master Hale. Tonight's my first time here. And so far it's amazing."

He held out his hand, and she returned the shake as he said, "Welcome. I hope you find your salvation here the way we all have." His wink was charming, even if there was a flatness to those black eyes peering at her through the silver metal.

"Thank you, Sir."

"We'll look for you all later?" Cruz asked. When the men nodded, they led her away again, down a long hallway off the main space lined with nondescript doors on both sides.

"These are all different play rooms," Master Jonathan said, leading her to one of the ones further down on the right. "And this one is ours for the night." He opened the door and gestured for her to enter.

Hartley's gaze didn't know what to focus on first. It was a luxuriously appointed bedroom, with nearly black hardwood floors covered here and there with shaggy red scatter rugs, dark red walls, a huge black leather couch, decorative iron scroll work upon the walls, and two gorgeous crystal chandeliers hanging from the ceiling. But none of that was what she most noticed.

First, a massive four-poster bed dominated one whole end of the rectangular space. A bed unlike any she'd ever seen before. The mattress sat at least three feet off the floor, and there was a single step to reach it—the height occasioned by the fact that, beneath the mattress platform, an iron railing ran all around the floor, creating some sort of…cage. A cage with pillows inside. Hooks, metal loops, chains, ropes, and straps were tucked away discretely here and there, and the footboard of the bed had holes in it—holes for heads, arms, and feet. Like a stocks.

And second, the whole wall alongside the bed was covered with toys of every kind. Leather, wood, glass, silicone. Whips, floggers, ropes, dildos, feathers. Some things she couldn't even identify. Hartley unleashed a shaky breath, suddenly hyper aware that her Masters were watching her. Swallowing, she turned to them, and found that they'd both removed their masks.

"Remember everything we talked about the other night?" Master Cruz asked, his voice dropping into that low, gritty tone she loved. "You may answer."

"Yes, Sir."

He nodded. "Then kneel."

Hartley's heart tripped into a sprint, because this was her first time playing with them like this. With them as her Doms, her Masters. And her as their submissive. It was a fucking rush already and they'd barely started. She gathered the chiffon of her skirt and sank to her knees, assuming the position they'd taught her the other night—ass against her heels, knees spread, straight posture, hands upward on her thighs.

"Eyes on me, Hartley," Master Jonathan said, his voice a low rasp. "God, I could look at you like that all damn night." He came closer, close enough that she had to tilt her head back to maintain eye contact. "We're going to take turns fucking your mouth." He unzipped his jeans, and his cock spilled free as he opened the placket.

Beside him, Master Cruz did the same, unfastening the fine material of his dress pants until his length also jutted out in front of her. She wanted to go to them. To pleasure them. But she'd paid attention to what Master Jonathan said. They were leading this.

"Open," Master Cruz said. "Open for your Masters' cocks."

Hartley dropped her jaw and kept her eyes on Jonathan as he guided his rock-hard erection to her mouth. He went slow at first, allowing her to bathe him with her saliva, and then he moved faster. Finally, he grasped her by the jaw and the back of the head, his hips really moving, his cock finding the back of her throat again and again.

And that was all it took for Hartley to be suddenly and totally wet between her legs.

Jonathan withdrew, and Cruz was right there, taking his turn with her mouth and taxing her with his impressive girth. Back and forth they went, their muttered curses and praise as arousing as the way they used her body for their pleasure.

When they both pulled free, Master Jonathan offered her a hand and helped her rise. "Turn around and lower your head. I'm going to undress you now so nothing happens to your gown." Hartley obeyed, aroused by the little touches of his fingers undoing the pearl button at the back of her neck and drawing down the side zipper. He peeled the fabric off her body. "Step out of it." She did that, too, which left her standing only in a black satin thong and a pair of sexy, strappy heels. And the lace mask that fit snugly against the contours of her face.

Master Cruz walked around her in a circle. Observing. Evaluating. Devouring her with his gaze. "Remove the panties. Slowly."

Her pulse set to a perpetual racing, Hartley grasped the thin scrap of silky material and slowly worked it over her hips and down her thighs, making a little show of it by bending down to remove them.

"Very nice," Master Jonathan said. "Now on the bed. On your knees, hands on the footboard." Her brain ran over the instructions, making sure she didn't miss a thing. But in doing so, she'd apparently hesitated, because Master's Jonathan's eyebrow raised in what struck her as a sexy threat.

And even though that was intriguing all by itself, Hartley moved. She carefully climbed the step, crawled onto the bed, and got into the position he commanded. When Master Cruz joined her, he was naked. And he had a bottle of lube in hand.

Meanwhile, Jonathan walked to the wall to peruse the toys, selecting a vibrating massager off a hook—and then he sat on the bed next to her leg and peered up at her. "Tonight, you're going to take both of us. But before you can have both of us, we want you to get used to having a cock in your ass. And if you can handle Master Cruz there, you can handle both of us."

Goosebumps broke out across Hartley's skin and she shivered.

"I think she likes that idea, Cruz," Master Jonathan said.

From behind her, Master Cruz tapped at the inside of her thigh, sending a jolt through her. "Wider." Hartley opened her knees. Then his hand fell on her back. "Down." She lowered her upper body. "Very good, Hartley," he said. And damn if the praise didn't warm her even more.

A buzzing sounded out, and then Master Jonathan moved the massager between Hartley's legs and placed it right against her clit. She cried out as the goodness of the sensation hit her, half worried that she'd be corrected for speaking. But they didn't say anything. Because Jonathan's fingers were at her ass, coating her with lube, inside and out.

She was nervous, even though they'd played with a bigger anal plug yesterday, and an even bigger one this morning when they'd all woken up in Jonathan's king-size bed. She just didn't want to do anything to disappoint them, and she desperately wanted to bring the three of them together this way.

"You're ready, Hartley," Master Cruz said, his voice full of grit. "Trust us to take care of you." She nodded.

"And you may now speak freely," Master Jonathan said, circling the massager over her clit. "Tell us your safe words."

Swallowing hard, Hartley repeated back to them what they'd taught her. "Green for good or go, yellow for slow down, and red for stop."

"Yes," Jonathan growled. "She's ready, Master Cruz."

Then Cruz's fat cock was right there, bare skinned just like they'd agreed two nights before when they'd all discussed their histories and the fact that she was on birth control. He lined his head up with her ass and pushed in with an incredible pressure that made Hartley feel like she needed to hold her breath. Cruz smacked her ass, sending a bolt of arousal through her. "Breathe, Hartley. And bear down. Invite me in."

She did what he asked, and more of his thickness invaded her. The stretching sensation was overwhelming—it stole her thoughts and her inhibitions and her very sanity. Hartley cried out, torn between the pleasure Master Jonathan forced upon her with the vibrator and the pain of Master Cruz's huge cock. It was a maddening combination, one that made her eyes sting with unshed tears at the sheer power of it.

"Almost there, baby," Cruz said, his hold tight on her hips. "Taking me so damn good."

Master Jonathan shifted onto his knees beside them, his free hand smoothing over her ass cheek. "What a good fucking girl you are, taking our Cruz that way."

God, their words helped, adding another layer of pleasure to the experience.

"It's so much," she cried, wiggling her hips.

Cruz spanked her again. "Be still."

The impact of his hand made her moan. "I think she needs more of that, Cruz," Jonathan said. "Don't you, Hartley? Don't you need to be spanked as your Master fucks your ass?"

"Yes, *please*."

Master Jonathan spanked her *hard*. "Yes, what?"

Oh, God. "Yes, *Sir*."

"That's right." He pressed the vibrator harder against her, making her cry out. And then his hand came down on her ass again. *Spank*.

"Fuck, I'm there, Jay. She took all of me. Just like we knew she could," Cruz rasped.

Spank. "That's our girl." *Spank*. "So fucking good." *Spank*. "Taking everything we give her." *Spank*.

Hartley had barely had time to adjust to the spanking with the vibrations with the incredible bone-bending fullness of Master Cruz's cock when he slowly withdrew. And that was a whole other riot of sensation. One that had her suddenly on the edge of coming.

"Oh, God, Master, I'm—"

He shoved back in, stealing her breath and her words. And shoving her body hard over the cliff of release. Hartley nearly screamed at the intensity of it, an intensity highlighted by the fact that her muscles were squeezing around such an incredible invasion.

"Again!" Master Jonathan growled. "As often as you can with his cock in your ass."

Cruz's pace picked up, his thickness threatening to split her in two, his hips pounding against her ass. But having come, her body registered all those sensations as entirely erotic—even if there was still some pain.

And as Cruz fucked her and Jonathan spanked and masturbated her, Hartley came again. And again. Until she was shoving back on his fat cock out of her own desire to be filled by him and to take every last inch.

"It's time," Cruz finally gritted out. Banding his arms around her waist, he hauled her against his chest, and then he laid both of them back against the bed, impaling her on his cock.

The moan Hartley unleashed was loud in the room because Jonathan had turned the vibrator off. He removed his jeans, his cock jutting long and hard in front of him as he climbed up the step to join them on the bed. But instead of laying, he stood between her and Cruz's legs. Stroking his cock as he loomed over them.

Hartley almost couldn't imagine how they could make this night any better than it had already been. But she was absolutely willing to let them try.

Standing over the two people who had become his whole life over the past four weeks, Jonathan stroked his cock, more aroused than he'd ever been before. Because this time was laden with emotion. Emotion that they'd all acknowledged, at least to some extent.

"You two look so hot I could get myself off to just the sight of you laying like that. Shoot my load all over you while you fuck each other in front of me." He shook his head. "Mmm. Another time." He got to his knees, and then he paused. "Where are you, Hartley? What color?"

She forced her gaze to his and gave him a smile. "Green, Sir."

Damn, she was doing so good, proving once again how right she was for them. "Making me so proud of you. You're doing great, you hear me?"

"Thank you, Sir," she whispered, her expression going soft at the praise.

Her sweetness made Jonathan need her even more. "It's time for the three of us to come together, all at once. Just like this."

"Fuck, Jay, you need to get in her," Cruz said, his hands moving over her breasts, her stomach, and reaching down to where Jonathan was lining his cock up at her pussy.

"Yes," Jonathan said, entering her and finding her tighter than ever before. But she was so wet that her slickness eased the way.

"Oh, my *God!*" she cried. "Ohmigod, ohmigod."

Jonathan released a harsh breath. "Where are you, darlin'?"

"Green. I'm green. It's so good but it's so much," she babbled.

"Take us, baby. Take both of us," Cruz rasped. "Do you feel that? Jonathan rubbing against me through you?"

Hartley's writhed. "Yes, I feel it. I feel everything." She reached a hand down to her clit.

Jonathan pushed her touch away. "Your orgasms are *ours* to give tonight." He grinned at her whimper, and then he was the one spilling a harsh groan of need, because he bottomed out inside her. She'd taken them all—of course, she'd really done that days ago when she'd taken their hearts. A realization that put words on the tip of his tongue. Words he hadn't yet said. But just then, Jonathan could only manage to say one thing. "*Hartley,*" he rasped.

"Move, please. I need to feel you move in me," she pleaded.

"God, she begs so pretty, Jonathan. Give her what she needs," Cruz said.

And they did. Jonathan withdrew, pulling a moan out of all of them. At the same time, Cruz thrust his hips, going deeper inside her ass. They alternated that way for long, decadently good minutes, and Jonathan reveled in Cruz's increasingly desperate groans and the wanton way Hartley thrust her own hips to meet each of their strokes.

Then Jonathan came down on top of them. He supported much of his weight on hands he braced beside Cruz's shoulders, not all of it. Because he wanted them to feel him as he fucked them—fucked them *both*. Because Cruz was right—the sensation of their cocks sliding and shifting together inside Hartley was insanely good.

"Ooh, that's good," Hartley said, meeting Jonathan's every thrust. He ground against her clit on every stroke, needing to feel her come again despite how many orgasms they'd wrung out of her already.

"You gonna come on our cocks, Hartley?" Jonathan asked. "Squeeze us both so hard until we're filling you up, too?"

"Yes," Hartley said, her voice full of strain. "I'm so close."

"Come, baby," Cruz said, her voice a raw scrape. "I'm right there. I can't… Fuck. *Fuck*, I'm coming." His hips jolting against them in a punctuated thrust.

And it set Hartley off next, making all three of them groan at the incredible pulsing tightness of her release. Jonathan was clenching his teeth and trying to hold on. But then Cruz lay his wrists right next to Jonathan's hands and spoke words that spelled doom to the last of his restraint.

Nailing Jonathan with a stare from behind Hartley's shoulder, Cruz said, "Hold my hands down and fuck us 'til you come."

Jonathan didn't hesitate, because the image was too hard to resist, let alone the reality of Cruz allowing him to do this. So he pinned his best friend's big hands down against the bed, and let his hips swing in fast, punctuated thrusts made more urgent by the sensation spiraling down his spine—and shooting out through his cock. Jonathan came on shout that echoed off the walls. He thrust through the wrenching pulses, his orgasm going on and on until he sagged on top of Hartley—on top of them both.

On a moan, he kissed her. Her eager hands in his hair held him there, stealing his breath and his heart all over again.

Forcing himself to his knees on the bed, he helped ease Hartley off of Cruz, and then he pulled her so that she straddled his thighs and he could hold her in his arms. "Such a good, good girl, Hartley. I'm so damn proud of you."

Cruz was right there with them, stroking her skin and pressing kisses against her back, her shoulder.

She turned her face so she could see them both. "That was the most intimate, soul-stirring thing I've ever done. Thank you for sharing it with me. I…" She swallowed hard.

"What, baby?" Cruz asked, kissing her cheek.

"I just…love you guys." Suddenly, she was blinking fast and her eyes were bright and glassy. "So much." She reached to put an arm around Cruz's shoulders, too.

Which had his best friend speaking next. "I do, too. Jonathan, I think I've loved you most of my life, even if that love is so much stronger today," Cruz said. "And Hartley, you've made me fall completely in love with you, even when I wasn't sure I should. But I do love you, baby girl. I really fucking do."

His friends kissed, and Jonathan's heart swelled in his chest. Because *this*…this was everything he'd ever hoped he might find. Which was why his throat was tight when he spoke. "Thank fuck," Jonathan managed, nearly overwhelmed with emotion as he pulled each of them in for a kiss of his own. "You two are everything to me. I love you, and I don't want to be apart from you. I want us like this, always."

Hartley burst into tears. "I…I don't know why I'm crying," she said, pressing a hand to her mouth. "I'm so *happy*."

"Subspace," Cruz said.

Jonathan nodded, satisfaction rolling through him. Because Hartley was more submissive than she even realized—capable of giving herself over, of surrendering, and therefore of opening herself up to the depth of emotion and sensation some submissives could experience. "We pushed her hard enough. Take her to the couch. I'll get you a blanket and some water."

Short minutes later, the three of them sat together on the couch, Hartley sitting in Cruz's lap, her head against his shoulder while Jonathan rubbed her feet.

"Where do we go from here?" she asked drowsily.

And it was a brave damn question, because admitting love was one thing, but turning that love into a working relationship was something else altogether.

"We'll figure it out together," Cruz said.

Jonathan nodded. "That we will. Because I promise you, tonight is just the beginning."

Epilogue

CRUZ STOOD AT THE HELM of the *Far 'n Away* and stared out at the wide blue horizon of the Chesapeake Bay. The view gave him hope, as if the whole future was wide open to him. To all of them. And it was. For the first time, he could really believe that.

His parents' disapproval still hurt like hell, but something had happened that gave him hope that they could still yet come around. This morning, Hartley's friend, Linda, the older lady who managed the marina office, had caught them at the docks before they'd set sail. She'd brought Hartley a birthday present—but the real gift had been that she'd teasingly asked Hartley what was going on between the three of them. And their Hartley—their brave, fearless girl—had *told* her that she was dating both him and Jonathan. Linda's expression had been almost comically gobsmacked by the news, but she'd recovered beautifully, not only smiling at the men and chiding them to take care of Hartley in that grandmotherly way she had, but also hugging Hartley and jokingly asking to let her know if they had any much older brothers.

If Linda could accept them, maybe his parents could, too. Someday. In the meantime, he had the love of two incredible people. Both of whom, through their words and their actions, were slowly but surely chasing away every last one of his fears.

Today had been another great day. It was Hartley's birthday, and all she'd asked for was to spend the day out on the water with her two favorite men. How much of a lucky fucker that Cruz was one of them? They'd cruised the bay, sailed past a few lighthouses, swam off the back of her boat, ate a delicious lunch under the autumn sky, and made love in the cabin they'd spent so much time repairing. It was damn near a perfect day.

"I guess we should head back soon," Hartley said, sitting perfectly still in the captain's chair.

"There's one thing we gotta do first," Jonathan said, sitting on the bench seat beside her.

Hartley smiled, her cheeks pink from the sun, her hair windblown around her face. She was absolutely gorgeous. "Oh, yeah? What's that?"

"Give me five minutes, then come down to the salon and see." Jonathan waggled his eyebrows at both of them, then disappeared.

Hartley arched a brow at him, and Cruz shrugged. "He's a devious motherfucker. I don't know."

Laughter spilled out of her. "Pot, meet kettle."

Bracing his arms on either side of the chair, Cruz boxed her in. "That's what you think, huh?"

"That's what I know," she said, her gaze all challenging.

Grinning, Cruz kissed her deeply, and it was a kiss filled with banked passion and deep emotion. Full of love, for him. "You know, I think you have thirty-one spanks coming your way sometime today."

Heat flashed through her eyes. "Well that sounds—"

"Yo, birthday girl," Jonathan called from inside. "Get your sexy ass in here."

She chuckled. "Let's go see this so-called deviousness."

Laughing, Cruz followed her into the salon where they found

the galley table covered with two little presents and a small chocolate cake with four lit candles atop it—three grouped together on one side, and a single one on the other. Cruz gave him a nod, because he *had* known about the cake—but not the extra gifts. He frowned. What was Jonathan up to now? They'd already given her presents this morning. Still laying in Hartley's bed, they'd presented her with a membership to the club, one of his framed photographs of a bald eagle over the bay, and a charm bracelet with a sailboat, a masquerade mask, a heart, and three colorful birthstone crystals representing each of them.

"Aw, you guys. You didn't need to do this." Her smile was as bright as the sun. "But I'm glad you did."

"Blow out the candles and make a wish," Jonathan said, his voice a little…off? Cruz eyeballed him and threw him a *what's up* expression. Jonathan gave a single shake of his head.

"Okay," Hartley said. "Here goes." For a long moment, she closed her eyes, and then she leaned down and blew them out. "And there are presents, too?"

Crossing his arms, Jonathan nodded. And Cruz almost would've sworn the guy was nervous.

Hartley grabbed the first little square box, and got the most comical expression on her face. "This one's for you, Cruz."

"Me?" He took it warily. Like he'd told her, devious motherfucker.

"And this one's for me." She clutched the matching box to her chest. "Let's open them together. Ready?"

Eyeing Jonathan, he nodded. And then they were both tearing the ribbon and pulling off the lid. Hartley gasped. And Jonathan's jaw dropped. Because if he'd ever worried about them wanting him for the long-term, this box had totally allayed that fear.

On top was a set of shiny silver keys on an engraved silver dog-tag-style keychain. It read *Far 'n Away II*. "What does yours say?" Cruz asked Hartley.

"*Far 'n Away I*," she said.

Jonathan pulled a matching set of keys from his pocket. "And mine says *Far 'n Away III*. They're the keys—"

"—to your condo," Cruz finished, recognizing the more beat-up keys on Jonathan's new ring.

"Yeah." Jonathan gave a fast nod. "I don't want to be apart from either of you, so…I'm inviting you to move in with me. Both of you. But there's more." He nodded toward the boxes.

Overwhelmed by the gesture and everything it said about their future, Cruz pulled out a folded square of paper and set his box aside. He unfolded it as Hartley opened hers.

It was a real estate listing. For a nearby house on the water. A *very private* house judging by the acreage and the neighborhood. Jesus, when had Jonathan done all this?

"I'm hoping, if you're both open to it, that my place would just be temporary. And that we could maybe find a house that we could all call home. I kinda fell in love with this one, but I'll look at as many houses as you two like if it means we could find one where we could build a life."

"A life together," Hartley said, her voice tight with emotion. "Oh, Jonathan. This is beautiful." She rushed into his arms.

And then the two of them looked to Cruz, who was clutching the key and the paper like they were lifelines. And he guessed maybe they were. "I worried you two wouldn't want me forever. That eventually you'd want to pair off."

"What?" Hartley exclaimed, her mouth falling open.

Whereas Jonathan's expression turned to a dark storm. "What the fuck, Cruz?"

He held up a hand. "I worried about that back at the *beginning*. But this…" He shook his head as the words lodged in his throat. "This proves just how wrong I was."

"Get over here," Hartley said, holding open her arm. Drawing them together the way she always did. "You're our family. We would never want to be without you."

As he joined their embrace, Cruz nodded, and Jonathan's hand cupped the back of his neck.

"I'm far and away happiest when I'm with you both," Jonathan said.

"Aw, that's why the keychains," Hartley said. Jonathan nodded. "This is my very best birthday. And I would love to move in with you."

"All I know is that I want to be wherever you both are," Cruz managed.

"Then it's settled," Jonathan said, deep satisfaction rolling over a sexy, aroused expression.

"It's settled," Cruz agreed.

"Yes," Hartley said, uttering that one word that had first brought them all together.

And together was right where they were going to stay. Because when you found people who accepted you for exactly who you were, you held on tight.

And you didn't let go.

And none of them would. Not ever.

Acknowledgements

I HOPE YOU ENJOYED THIS NEWEST story in the Blasphemy series! And I hope you'll join my VIP Readers – because I'd love to share all kinds of fun exclusives with you!

I had my own saviors while writing this book. Namely my very good author friends, Christi Barth and Lea Nolan, who selflessly threw themselves into editing and proofreading and helping me make Hartley, Jonathan, and Cruz's story shine. I love these ladies like sisters and appreciate all they do for me so much.

I must also thank KP Simmon, who is always such an amazing source of support, but who was a cheerleader and a protector and a generator of fun ideas around this book.

One of the best parts of writing *Theirs to Take* was all the amazing encouragement I received from readers while writing it. You guys might not realize the impact your posts and notes have, but each and every *I can't wait for this book!* I received pushed me through when the going got tough – thank you!

This book would not have been finished without the patience of my kids, who encouraged me to go work and cheered me on when I finished. My family is an amazing source of support, and I couldn't do what I love without them.

Or without all of you. Thanks, as always, to my Heroes and my Reader Girls. And thank YOU, dear reader, for taking my characters into your heart and allowing them to tell their stories over and over again.

~LK

Need more Masters???

GET THE WHOLE BLASPHEMY SERIES – AN EROTIC ROMANCE SERIES OF STANDALONES…

From the ruins of a church comes Baltimore's most exclusive club
12 Masters. Infinite Fantasies.
Welcome to Blasphemy…

BOOKS IN SERIES:
HARD TO SERVE
BOUND TO SUBMIT
MASTERING HER SENSES
EYES ON YOU
THEIRS TO TAKE

COMING IN 2018:
ON HIS KNEES
SWITCHING FOR HER

HARD TO SERVE
(HARD INK #5.5/BLASPHEMY #.5)

To protect and serve is all Detective Kyler Vance ever wanted to do, so when Internal Affairs investigates him as part of the new police commissioner's bid to oust corruption, everything is on the line. Which makes meeting smart, gorgeous submissive, Mia Breslin, at an exclusive play club the perfect distraction. Their scorching scenes lure them to play together again and again. But then Kyler runs into Mia at work and learns that he's been dominating the daughter of the hard-ass boss who has it in for him. Now Kyler must choose between life-long duty and forbidden desire before Mia finds another who's not so hard to serve.

BOUND TO SUBMIT (BLASPHEMY #1) – FREE ON ALL RETAILERS

He thinks he caused her pain, but she knows he's the only one who can heal her... Kenna Sloane lost her career and her arm in the Marines, and now she feels like she's losing herself. Submission is the only thing that ever freed her from pain and made her feel secure, and Kenna needs to serve again. Bad. The only problem is the Dom she wants once refused her submission and broke her heart, but, scarred on the inside and out, she's not looking for love this time. She's not even sure she's capable. Griffin Hudson is haunted by the mistakes that cost him the only woman he ever loved. Now she's back at his BDSM club, Blasphemy, and more beautiful than ever, and she's asking for his help with the pain he knows he caused. Even though he's scared to hurt her again, he can't refuse her, because he'd give anything to earn a second chance. And this time, he'll hold on forever.

MASTERING HER SENSES (BLASPHEMY #2)

He wants to dominate her senses—and her heart... Quinton Ross has always been a thrill-seeker—so it's no surprise that he's drawn to extremes in the bedroom and at his BDSM club, Blasphemy, where he creates sense-depriving scenarios that blow submissives' minds. Now if he could just find one who needs the rush as much as him... Cassia Locke hasn't played at Blasphemy since a caving accident left her with a paralyzing fear of the dark. Ready to fight, she knows just who to ask for help—the hard-bodied, funny-as-hell Dom she'd always crushed on—and once stood up. Quinton is shocked and a little leery to see Cassia, but he can't pass up the chance to dominate the alluring little sub this time. Introducing her to sensory deprivation becomes his new favorite obsession, and watching her fight fear is its own thrill. But when doubt threatens to send her running again, Quinton must find a way to master her senses—and her heart.

EYES ON YOU
(BLASPHEMY #3)

She wants to explore her true desires, and he wants to watch... When a sexy stranger asks Wolf Henrikson to rescue her from a bad date, he never expected to want the woman for himself. But their playful conversation turns into a scorching one-night stand that reveals the shy beauty gets off on the idea of being seen, even if she's a little scared of it, too. And Wolf loves to watch. In the wake of discovering her fiancé's infidelity, florist Olivia Foster never expected to find someone who not only understood her wildest, darkest fantasies, but would bring them to life. As Wolf introduces her to his world at the play club, Blasphemy, Liv finds herself tempted to explore submission and exhibitionism with the hard-bodied Dom even as she's scared to trust again. But Wolf is a master of getting what he wants—and he's got his eyes set on her...

Introducing

REVEAL ME
(A Steele Brothers Novella)
By
Jennifer Probst

A Special Crossover Release with Laura's
THEIRS TO TAKE
If you want to know more about Leonardo and Scarlett, read on, then grab the book!

Chapter One

LEONARDO SINCLAIR STEPPED INTO THE cool darkness and swept his gaze over the soaring, vaulted ceiling of the converted church. Colorful frescoes decorated the walls and thick marble columns lined the open area. Massive stained-glass windows offered protection from the curious gazes and judgments of the outside world. A smile touched his lips as he took a deep breath. Damn, it'd been a long time since he indulged in his favorite vices.

Good thing he'd come to Blasphemy for play rather than forgiveness for his many sins. The popular Baltimore BDSM club was everything he'd hoped it would be, and he intended to enjoy every moment before it was time to head to Vegas.

Adjusting the plain black mask he wore, he moved forward, appreciating the large circular bar made of gleaming marble and the intimate set up of leather couches, chairs, and private nooks where couples gathered to chat and play. The sexy timbers of hip-hop ground out from the speakers and urged crowds onto the dance floor. He savored the scents of musk, sweat, and sex drifting in the air, heading toward the bar. He usually hated themed parties such as a masquerade ball, but when one of his brothers from his Navy days asked him to do something, he did it. So when Jonathan and Cruz had invited him to the party before he put the East Coast behind him, he'd agreed.

Now, he was glad. The muscles in his neck and shoulders began to soften from the long car drive. He'd grab a drink, try to find his buddies, and play with a sweet subbie tonight. Someone easy and experienced. Someone he'd enjoy for a few hours in mutual satisfaction and never look back on. Someone—

"About time you got here," the familiar voice called out.

He turned around with a grin, shaking his head at the wolf mask covering the top half of Jonathan's face. "Got stuck in traffic. Please don't tell me I'm supposed to be channeling some sort of animal here?"

"Like an ass? Nah, you're good. Let's just say I'm in the mood to hunt tonight."

Leo laughed and they embraced. Jonathan's quick wit and humor made for an easy friendship, but it was his fierce loyalty and work ethic that earned Leo's respect. With his staggering height and long blonde hair, he had a quiet presence that screamed authority. "Is there a particular target you have in mind?" Leo asked. "Or is it an open field?"

Jonathan's gaze narrowed thoughtfully. "Oh, there's a target. Her name is Hartley. Tonight's her first time at Blasphemy."

"Sounds promising. Cruz on board?"

"You better believe it," another voice said from his left. Leo turned, recognizing Cruz's short, dark hair and tattoos over warm brown skin even beneath the smooth, famously carved white mask. Shorter than Jonathan, he had bulging muscles that either had a woman running in fear or begging for more. They clapped shoulders, and a fierce wave of emotion clipped through him. He'd forgotten how much he missed his friends. It had been too long.

Leo raised his brow. "Are you supposed to be the lamb to his wolf?"

Cruz winked. "Wouldn't you like to know? Besides, gotta keep her guessing. Much more fun that way, as you've told us many times."

They all laughed. Leo waved his hand in the air. "This is amazing. I can't believe you're both part owners of this place."

"We'll introduce you to the other Masters later," Cruz said. "Now that we have the boat building and restoration business under control, we're able to enjoy ourselves a bit more. The people at Blasphemy have become a second family to us."

"I'm glad, you deserve it." After the Navy, they'd all struggled with finding the right fit and place to settle down. The military seemed the only thing that could temporarily satisfy his innate restlessness—always pushing him toward the next adventure. It was good Jonathan and Cruz seemed to find their fit here in Baltimore. Maybe he'd finally find his same place in Vegas. God knows, his cousins had been on his ass for years to go out and join them.

Cruz motioned him over. "Come on, I'll get you a whisky and we'll show you around."

"Sounds good."

They moved past the dance floor and deeper into the club, unveiling specialized theme rooms that catered to every dark, delicious whim, and a beautiful high platformed stage for various demonstrations. Leo crossed his arms and watched a willowy blonde floating above her Dom, her naked body bound with intricate rope work that offered her up like an artistic sacrifice. Low moans broke from her lips, and her body shook and shivered under her Dom's flick of the whip.

The crowd surrounding them was respectfully silent, yet caught up in the sensual tension ready to explode before them. Leo enjoyed the tight feel of skin over his bones, and the low punch of heat in his gut that preceded the anticipation of mastering an open, willing female. He'd always known he needed more in his sexual relationships, even young. The deep satisfaction of pleasuring another, of stripping away the walls and bullshit to get to the core—to become truly free with another—that's what kept him coming back to BDSM.

"Your wristband marks you as an experienced Dominant," Jonathan said, walking back toward the bar section. "All the subs have color coded bands that mark their limits and experience level. You're free to roam and pick from the crowd and all rooms are available for your use—we've already approved you for full access. We're using the masquerade theme to build membership, encourage more of the newbies to participate, and hopefully push some soft limits. Masks must stay on at all times. It's up to the individuals at the end of the session if they want to exchange true identities."

"Thanks. Honestly? This is one of the nicest clubs I've seen. You two have done good."

Jonathan nodded, pride shining in his eyes through the mask. "You still have to head out tomorrow?" he asked. "We were hoping you could stay with us for a few days."

"Appreciate it, but the new job starts and I want to get settled in."

"No better place than Vegas to bust some criminals. Who would've thought a math nerd could be so in demand for gambling?" Cruz smirked.

Leo laughed. "It was either DC or Sin City. Guess which one is a better fit?" His math talent had started young, and he'd learned early he could make buckets of money by gambling. Until he got busted by the casino's highly-paid security boss. Instead of a hospital visit or getting black balled, they offered him a job in Atlantic City. It fit his needs for a while until the restlessness hit again, and he enlisted in the Navy. His cousins were all poker dealers settled in Vegas, and had already set him up with a job. The idea of being around family called to him. He'd been alone for too many years, relying on his service buddies, but he missed his cousins and felt ready to stay in one place for a while.

Jonathan gave a mock shudder. "It may be good for sin, but I wouldn't be caught dead in the desert. No water, no beach, and no boats. Sounds like the devil's terrain to me."

Cruz rolled his eyes. "You can take the surfer dude out of California, but you can't take California out of the man."

Leo chuckled. "I get it. But the pay is good, the air conditioning is cold, and the women are hot. Plus, I need a new challenge. The casino has been getting jacked lately and they think I can make the bust. Could be fun."

"No doubt you'll do it. And if you get bored, you always have a place here," Jonathan said, clapping him on the back.

He nodded. "That means a lot."

"Any idea what type of submissive you're looking for tonight?" Cruz asked curiously.

"Been a while since I've indulged," he admitted. "I'm open to all possibilities, as long as the woman understands it's one night with no strings."

"Good, cause we'd like to introduce you to someone. Someone we think you'd enjoy," Cruz said. The man's dark eyes practically glinted with conspiracy and the zeal of a set-up. Cruz had always had a hidden soft side underneath that hard-assed demeanor.

"Trying to play matchmaker?" He cocked his head and studied his friends. "Or keeping me away from your sweet thing so she doesn't fall for me and dump you two?"

Cruz snorted. "Dream on."

Jonathan grinned. "She's a friend of Hartley's. I'd like to hook her up with someone I can trust. She's newer to the lifestyle. Only been a member for the past few months and hasn't played often. I think you'd get along."

Leo considered, then shrugged. His friends knew his tastes well, and though he usually preferred experienced subs, introducing a newbie into his world was always a fun challenge. "Sure."

Cruz and Jonathan exchanged a satisfied look. Interesting. His friends weren't the matchmaking types.

He wondered if this Hartley was the cause, and hoped it was. They both deserved happiness. They'd gone to the Naval Academy together, were partners in the boat building business, and liked to share women. It was hard to settle down with a woman who'd be a good match for both of them, and open to a ménage situation.

God knows, he couldn't find that type of connection and he was only one Dom, not two.

Jonathan's gaze sharpened past his right shoulder and a slow smile tugged his lips. "Speak of the devil," he murmured. "Here she comes."

Leo turned. Then froze.

Holy shit.

He'd been an experienced Dom for almost a decade, and not once had he felt the earth beneath his feet shift. He was known for his control and tight rein on his emotions. He didn't believe in star-struck first love, gazes meeting across a crowded room, or anything that stunk of sugar spun romance that held no depth.

Until now.

His damn tongue was stuck to the roof of his mouth. Were his eyes bugging out like a horn dog pre-teen? If his reaction hadn't been so surprising, he'd be humiliated. First impressions were critical during an initial Dom and Sub meet, and he'd just committed a newbie mistake. Staring at her like a love-struck school boy gave her the upper hand. Fuck—he'd never live this down.

"Leo, this is Hartley Farren, and her friend Scarlett Rose. Ladies, you may address Leo as Sir since he is not a Blasphemy Master."

They gave him a respectful nod, Hartley in an intricately patterned soft black mask that covered her eyes and nose and extended down unevenly over her cheeks. It almost appeared more tattoo than lace. And Scarlett in a more traditional sparkling black-and-red cut-out mask that made her eyes appear huge.

Still unable to communicate, he concentrated on Hartley and tried to get his shit together. Hartley smiled sweetly, a nice blush of color on her cheeks as she greeted him. Her sideswipe look at Jonathan and Cruz told him everything he needed to know. The little subbie was just as intoxicated with his friends as they were for her. He managed to murmur a greeting and say a quick prayer of thanks Hartley wasn't the one who had him tongue-tied. No, it was the woman standing quietly at her side who snagged his full attention.

Everything about her seemed like a contradiction. Though she stood completely still, an intense energy pulsed from her aura, reminding him of a downed live wire, crackling in sharp, intermittent bursts. Coal black hair fell almost to her waist in wild waves, untamed and made for his fingers to fist and pull. Inky dark eyes met his gaze directly, without a shred of shyness or hesitation. Framed by lush lashes, they tilted slightly outwards like a cat, emphasizing the angled cut of the simple black mask that hid half of her face. Her lips were full, and painted in the color of her name—a bold slash of blood-red.

His gaze probed; studied; analyzed. Her outfit was pure temptation. A skimpy red slip in shiny satin. Dipping low in the front, her cleavage teased him, and the fabric clearly showed her hard nipples. Her skin was pale, smooth, and looked soft to the touch. She was all ripe curves—ass and breasts and hips, and his fingers itched to touch and hurt and soothe. It looked as if she'd been about to get dressed, then decided to go out as is. The kicker was something so simple, probably not many Doms would notice.

Her bare feet.

Most women enjoyed wearing stilettos or fuck-me shoes at a club. Besides feeling sexy, it gave them a sense of power and height. He'd always been more turned on by the vulnerability and bravery of no shoes. If she was indeed new to BDSM, her choice indicated an almost rebellious courage that stiffened his cock and sped up his heart rate.

How long had it been since a woman struck him speechless? *Never.*

His continued silence must have urged her to speak. "It's nice to meet you, Sir," she said. Her words were slow and deliberate, with a husky smokiness that curled at the edges. Damned if he couldn't wait to hear her beg him in that delicious voice.

Finally, words sprung free from his throat. "The pleasure's mine. I hear we're both new to Blasphemy."

"Yes, Sir. I joined two months ago," Scarlett said, her eyes still on him. Right where he wanted them.

"And what about you, Hartley?" he asked with a smile.

"Scarlett spoke so highly of the club, she helped convince me to give it a try," Hartley said, chewing her bottom lip. "Now I'm just hoping I don't mess anything up."

Jonathan took her hand. "You're not doubting that we'll guide you every step of the way, are you?"

"Oh, no. I mean, no, Sir," she said.

"Maybe we need to show her exactly what that means," Cruz said, his voice full of dark, sensual promise.

Jonathan nodded and tugged Hartley between them. "Mmm, maybe we do."

Leo studied Scarlett. She seemed amused by the interaction, not fretful, which told him she was comfortable enough to know Cruz and Jonathan would never hurt Hartley.

Leo nodded. "Apology accepted. I promise I'll take very good care of Scarlett if we decide to play. And it seems your Masters will make sure you think before speaking in Blasphemy."

"Come with us, little one," Cruz commanded. "It's time for your first lesson."

"Lesson?" Hartley asked, dark eyes going wide.

Jonathan flanked her other side, guiding them away. "No speaking unless asked a direct question. Leo, Scarlett, I'll check in with you later. Have fun."

His friends left them alone amidst the squeak of leather and hiss of whip; the grinding music and clink of glasses; the smell of sex and sweat hanging thickly in the air.

Leo waited. He figured she'd either chatter, step back nervously, or dive right in with questions. And once again, she surprised him.

She said nothing.

Those Gypsy eyes stared back, not with challenge, but with patience. Waiting for him to lead. Waiting for him to speak first. She may be a newbie, but Scarlett had already pleased him faster than some of the more experienced women he'd played with in the past.

Oh, he was going to enjoy the evening very much.

"I'd like us to get to know one another before we discuss play. Would you like to go talk?" He offered his hand with an invitation she was completely free to decline.

Her gaze assessed him. He watched the thoughts flicker across her face, noting she had a mind that preferred logic to emotion. Fact and figures trumped impulse. He'd spent years in the lifestyle studying women and their thought patterns, finding how each unique personality needed a particular type of play for maximum effect. He'd begun to wonder if the scientific game of figuring them out had become more important than the physical aspect. Damn depressing, but this woman had already pushed his buttons without saying anything. Perhaps, there was something more here.

She reached out and took his hand, allowing him to lead her to the private area away from the main activity of the club. He chose a room that reminded him of a library, comfortable with the dark leather chairs, thick burgundy carpeting, and bookshelves filling up the far wall. An antique light burned low on the desk, wrapping them in dark intimacy. The room was perfect for playing naughty secretary, and the quick image of her sprawled on the desk, her bare bottom lifted for the slap of his hand, burned his vision.

She lowered herself onto the sofa, the short hem of her slip hiking up past her thighs. Her skin was pale and smooth. He couldn't wait to see the contrast of his darker skin against hers, sliding in between those gorgeous plump thighs to pleasure her.

As if she caught his thought, her breath hitched, so low he barely heard. Her fingers tugged the hem down in a display of nerves, before settling back into her quiet intensity.

Yes. This woman would be fun to watch shatter. Now he needed to find out how deep her control really went.

"I'd like to begin with some questions. I ask them so I can get all the important information to decide what you're looking for and what you need tonight."

"Don't you believe I already know what I need?"

Her voice reminded him of classic Lauren Bacall—growly, sexy, and deep. Already, her intellectual challenge told him her brain was usually in control of her body. His favorite type of woman to play with. "No. Many times a sub thinks she knows, but her Dom sees something more. How much do you know about BDSM?"

"I started with research from books and the Internet. Then I took the orientation at Blasphemy. I've been a member for a few months."

Good, at least she had some hands-on experience. He'd met way too many women turned on by erotic romance and diving into the club scene without realizing what was fact and what was fiction. Safety was always priority number one.

"Have you scened often?"

She stiffened. "No. Just twice."

His brow quirked. "Why?"

She considered him before giving an answer. Beneath her inexperience lay a touch of a brat—one of his favorite types. She seemed to naturally want to challenge a Dom. He'd need to use a firm hand. "I didn't really connect with the Doms."

Interest piqued. "Did they push too hard? Force you to say your safe word?"

She shook her head. "No, the opposite. I was frustrated after the session. During my orientation, I dealt with the Masters which I found more satisfying."

Hmm, she probably played with newer dominants and couldn't forge a connection. "Did you try to communicate your frustration to them? Tell them what you wanted from the experience?"

"It wasn't their fault they couldn't get me off."

Interesting. Her tone held a touch of hostility, contradicting her words. There was something deeper going on and he intended to figure it out. "Some matches don't work out, just like in the vanilla world. Your Dom is responsible for giving you pleasure, and it's not your fault if you weren't satisfied. Unless, of course, you kept something important from him. Was that the case?"

She shook her head.

"Then we'll need to remedy that experience."

She nodded, but he glimpsed the flare of doubt in her dark eyes. He lowered his voice in warning. "Since you are aware of the club rules, I'll expect to hear 'Yes or No Sir' or we'll need to begin our session with punishment."

Those red lips opened in a tiny O, then snapped close. "Yes, Sir."

"What do you do, Scarlett?"

"I'm a statistician. I've worked for the government the past five years but I'm moving to the private sector."

His interest peaked. A math nerd and a submissive. A heady combination. He, too, loved the calming effect of numbers and solving the puzzles they offered to understand the world. It was hard finding people who became passionate about the beauty of mixing simplicity with complexity through math. He bet she had issues shutting off that powerful mind and concentrating on her body. He made a mental note.

"I notice you haven't checked off many hard limits for a beginner." Her bracelets clearly showed she was open to pretty much anything, including sex. "You're open to pain. Flogger, spanking, cane, whip? Preferences?"

"I was told while I experimented with my threshold I could always use the club's safe word—red—or yellow, to slow down."

He nodded, pleased. "Correct. Since we're only playing tonight, I'll concentrate on core basics rather than testing limits. That's for your future Dom to decide during your training. Do you agree?"

"Yes, Sir."

"And sex is on the table?"

Not even a slight blush marred her pale cheek. "Yes, sir."

His cock twitched. He tamped down on his arousal and concentrated on the conversation. Plenty of time for his little head later. "Tell me about your background. I'd like to make sure you have no triggers."

"I don't." He arched his brow in warning. "I mean, I don't, Sir."

"It wasn't a question, Scarlett. I never go into a play session without feeling comfortable about my sub. This is for safety—for both of us."

Her chin tilted up slightly. Definitely defensive. Definitely a secret there he was dying to probe. "I'm divorced. It became a bit rocky at the end, but it's been a year now so I've worked through it. I went to therapy, so you won't have any surprises."

Admiration cut through him. He always believed everyone should get counseling just to get through life's pitfalls but it took guts to ask for help. "I'm sorry. Did you engage in BDSM play with your husband?"

"No, Sir."

She didn't seem to want to expand, so he pushed further. "Light bondage? Blindfold? Role play? Anything?"

"No, Sir."

Her stark admission told him more than he needed. Though he wanted more, he was pretty damn sure her ex hadn't been into bedroom kink and it had eventually become a problem. He studied her stiff body and distant eyes. No, this wasn't the way to go into their first session. She needed to be open to the experience or he'd be fighting ghosts he wasn't sure of. Going with his gut, he dove for the jugular.

"Little one, I understand it's hard to spill your innermost stuff to someone who's a stranger, but in under an hour, you're going to be naked, wet, and coming on my tongue. We could do this the hard way, or the easy way. The more I know about what you want and are looking for tonight, the better it will be. Use the mask as a tool to allow yourself to take the leap. But also know, I will strip away not only your clothes, but all those walls you've built to protect yourself. Now, make your decision."

Shock flared in her dark eyes, before quickly becoming masked. But she didn't duck her chin or try to hide. He watched her mentally step back and recalculate. Leo didn't know if she was ready to dive deep yet, but he sensed if he didn't push, they both may regret it later. Sex wasn't just an orgasm or feeling good for a few minutes. It was the biggest mind fuck of all—because it started with the brain, and who a person was at the very core. The right type of sex took all that mess, twisted it up, and released it hard and fast, like the crack of a champagne cork. Afterward, both body and mind were cleaner. Quieter.

Saner.

And that type of sex could never be boring.

Especially with this woman.

But he'd pushed harder than with others, and could have blown the whole damn thing. If she was an intellectual, she may not be able to let herself take the leap and tell him. Maybe he'd---

"I was married for three years to a man who slowly eroded everything I originally liked about myself."

Leo stilled. She spoke with a steady calm, but he caught the slight tremor in her body. Moving on pure instinct, he tangled his fingers with hers, offering her warmth, squeezing slightly in comfort. Damned if she wasn't tearing down every preconceived notion about what she'd be able to handle. This type of raw truth was rare this early on, and he'd make damn sure she felt supported. "Tell me about it, little one."

Her fingers squeezed back, accepting his offering. "I didn't think it was wrong to want more out of sex. Oh, sure, we started with vanilla, which was fine, but after the first year, I realized I craved other things. Dirty things. When I brought it up, he was shocked. Began telling me I was messed up to ask him to spank me, or tie me up. I tried to let it go, but my need kept getting worse. I tried talking to him. Asked him to experiment."

"He didn't want to?"

She shook her head. "Over time, I had to fake my arousal, but he could tell. I think it made him feel like less of a man, and he started taking it out on me. First, it was my weight. I was too big, not sexy enough for him to want me. Called me fat and useless. Then it poured out in all aspects of our life together. From how I did my job, to how I cleaned the house, and everything in between. I was a failure of a wife. I was a failure at turning him on. It went on and on. And finally, one day I realized I didn't even know who I was anymore. I looked in the mirror and saw nothing. Or at least, nothing I liked."

Anger thrummed in his veins, heating his blood. Oh, if he could bash her ex's face in, he'd be over the fucking moon. Typical shit. His ego got threatened so he took it out on his wife. "Sounds like you were strong enough to realize he has a serious condition."

She cocked her head. Inky waves spilled over her right cheek and tumbled over her shoulder. The scent of citrus drifted to his nostrils. Clean. Tangy. Sharp. Like her. "Condition?" she asked.

"Yeah, your ex is a true asshole." He relished her smile, then leaned into her space. The air between them crackled to life, twisting tight with a delicious sexual tension that couldn't be forced. Oh, his hands itched to get all over those gorgeous curves and show her how sexy they were. "Damned if you haven't impressed the hell out of me, Scarlett Rose. First, you were strong enough not to let him win. To claim who you were and walk away. Second, you were brave enough to tell me the truth. That's a woman I want to be with. A woman I want to give excruciating pleasure to with my mouth and tongue and teeth. Tie her up with her thighs spread wide and fuck her till she begs for mercy. Spank her ass till she's dripping wet and hot." Her pupils dilated at his words. "Would you like that?"

"Yes, Sir." This time, her words came out ragged. He raked his glance over her tight nipples, and noted her rapidly racing pulse. Citrus mingled with the musky smell of arousal. She liked the dirty talk. Good, cause so did he.

"Then our play will begin. Call me Sir at all times. Use the word yellow to slow things down. Red if you want things to stop completely."

"Yes, Sir."

"Don't be afraid to use it. Gaze lowered as I lead you to our room. No
speaking unless spoken to." He studied her lush body, allow-

ing a slight smile to rest on his lips. He hadn't looked this forward to a session in too long.

"Shall we begin?"

READ ON FOR A SNEAK peek at the next standalone romance in Laura's sexy and suspenseful Raven Riders series...

The Raven Riders MC

Brotherhood. Club. Family.
They live and ride by their own rules.
These are the Raven Riders . . .

RIDE WILD

Chapter 1

IT WAS THEIR NORMAL ROUTINE, and it was awkward as crap. Cora Campbell bit back a smile as she sat in the passenger seat of the beat-up pickup truck. She didn't think Sam Evans, her boss-of-sorts, would appreciate her humor. Or, like, *any* humor. He filled the driver's seat beside her, his big hands on the wheel and black tattoos snaking all down his lean, muscled arms. From the corner of her eye, she sneaked a glance at his face, and one word came to mind.

Wild.

Longish wild brown hair, like he couldn't keep from raking at it in frustration. Wild brown beard that Cora sometimes imagined chopping off just so she could better see the face it seemed like he purposefully hid beneath it. Pale green eyes, mesmerizing in their uniqueness, but also wild with emotions at which she could only guess . . .

"So, um, Slider," she said, her use of the nickname his motorcycle club had given him slicing through the uneasy silence, "anything special I need to know about Sam and Ben for tonight?"

That pale gaze slashed her way, and she felt the chill of it into her bones. Slider didn't scare her—he was too good to his boys for that. But it was entirely possible that his glances appeared in the dictionary next to *Intimidating as Fuck*. And maybe even *If Looks Could Kill*. And definitely *Like, Whoa*. It was a good thing he paid her so well to babysit his sons. In truth, he was doing her a pretty big favor giving her a part-time job while she figured out her life, so she put up with his . . . moodiness.

He huffed out a breath, as if mustering the energy to reply sucked vital life force from his soul or something. "Sam has homework he wants your help with," he said, his tone almost apologetic. "And Ben . . . is Ben."

Cora nodded. Having babysat the kids four or five days a week for the past three months, she had a decent idea what Slider meant. At six, Ben was a sweetheart of a boy, but nightmares and monsters under the bed gave him more than a little difficulty sleeping. "Okay."

They came upon the two-story white farmhouse where Slider lived and she sometimes worked. Empty, overgrown flower beds. A misshapen wreath on the door, so bleached from the sun Cora could no longer tell what color it'd originally been. Shutters hanging at odd angles from years of neglect. The house had an abandoned, decaying feel about it, and Cora didn't really have to wonder why that was.

Slider hadn't even parked when the front door exploded open, the creaky screen door wobbling like it might just give up and fall off its hinges. A little boy darted out next to the gravel driveway, hopping excitedly as if the grass hid a trampoline. Except for the lighter brown hair and happiness shaping his face, there was no denying Ben was Slider's kid.

Cora stepped out of the truck into the warm early September evening wearing a smile. "Hey, jumping bean."

"Name's Ben, not Bean," he said, his grin all the cuter for the big gap where his front teeth should've been.

"You sure? I could've sworn it was Bean." She hugged him as he threw his arms around her waist. Where Slider was a walking, talking wall that kept all his emotions barricaded, his younger son wore every single emotion on his sleeve.

"No." He laughed. "It's *Ben!*"

"Okay, Bean." Hiking up the backpack that served as an overnight bag, she glanced at Slider and found him watching her through narrowed eyes, like maybe she was a foreign language he couldn't decipher. Tall and broad-shouldered, he had a ranginess about him that, like the house, spoke of neglect. She'd seen him sit with the kids at meals, sometimes even with a plate of food in front of him. But it was possible she'd eaten more watching movies in bed with her friends Haven and Alexa last weekend than she'd seen Slider eat in the past three months combined.

The youngest Evans let loose a long-suffering groan. "No, Cora, it's *Ben*," he said, pronouncing her name more like *Coowa*. It was so cute it almost killed her.

"Finally, you're here," Sam called from the front door. At ten going on eleven going on thirty-five, the kid was the definition of an old soul. It was in his eyes, the seriousness of his personality, the way he took care of his little brother, as if, without being asked, he was trying to relieve some of the burden of being a single parent from his father's shoulders.

"I am, in fact, here. Now the party can begin," Cora said, ruffling the older boy's hair as she stepped into the neat but shabby living room. Sam tried to hold back his smile as he dodged her hand, but didn't quite manage.

"Wait. We're having a party?" Ben asked as she dropped her bag on the couch.

Sam rolled his eyes. "No, doofus, it's an expression."

Ben's shoulders fell, and now Cora was the one holding back a smile. "If two certain someones I know take their showers without any complaints, maybe, just maybe, we can have a party." The littler boy's grin was immediate, but what really caught her attention was the way that Sam's attention perked up, even though he tried to hide it. "Deal?" she asked.

Just as both boys agreed, Slider cleared his throat.

Cora turned to find him shrugging into his button-up uniform shirt with its *Frederick Auto Body and Repair* logo, the movement causing his T-shirt to ride up his side. Just a momentary glance. Just of one small part of his body. But it revealed two things that stole her breath—more ink, and a frame that was all raw muscle and sinew.

Like a wild animal.

The comparison should've been alarming, but for some reason, that wasn't how her body interpreted it if the flutter in her belly was any indication. Never in a million years would she have described Slider as attractive, but there was something unquestionably *attracting* about him, even if she couldn't quite articulate what that was.

"Leaving?" she managed.

He nodded. "On seven to seven," he said. "You have my cell."

"We'll be fine," she said, bracing her hands on Ben's shoulders. "Won't we?" she asked, hugging him against her as she peered down into his little face.

"Yeah," he said. "Don't worry, Dad."

Slider gave a single nod as his gaze skated between Cora and his sons. "See ya later, alligators."

Sam rolled his eyes, but Ben grinned and said, "After while, crocodile."

Slider winked at his youngest. Just a single little wink. But, together with the way he said good-bye to the kids every time he left, it proved to Cora that there was a sweet, playful man in there somewhere. Or at least there used to be.

Either way, it was clear that what Slider had left of himself to give, he gave to his boys. And given what a miserable piece of crap both her dad and her best friend's father had been, Cora knew how much having a good father mattered. It mattered a lot. She had to respect that much about Slider, whatever else his faults might be.

The door had barely closed behind her boss when Ben whirled on her. "Is it time for the party yet?"

"No," Sam said, looking a little nervous. "I, uh, I have homework first."

"Later, kiddo. I promise. Why don't you watch some TV while I get dinner on?" When Ben made for the family room at the back of the house, Cora eyeballed Sam. "Your dad said you wanted help. That right?"

"Yeah." He shifted feet, like something about wanting her help made him uncomfortable.

"Okay, well, why don't you work at the table while I make us some food?" she suggested, leading them into the kitchen, where the neat but shabby theme continued. "How's pasta sound?"

Sam shrugged as he slid into a seat and slapped a worn-out backpack onto the table, appearing every inch like a prisoner being led to the gallows.

"What's up with you?" Cora asked as she crumbled ground beef into a frying pan to brown. Next, she filled a big pot of water to boil.

He sighed. "I have to do an interview."

Frowning, she pulled a jar of sauce and a box of noodles from the pantry. She was going to need to ask Slider to grab some groceries soon, a chore that would be so much easier if she had a car of her own. As would getting back and forth to watch the boys. Cora sighed. Just one more thing to add to her list of stuff she really needed to make happen in her life. "Of?"

"Someone I admire." He stared at the page in his hand.

Wiping her hands on a towel, she turned to him. "Okay, and did you have someone in mind?"

He looked up at her. And even though he didn't say a word, his eyes held the answer.

Suddenly, Cora was the uncomfortable one, which had her

rambling. "Um, maybe, like Doc? Or Bunny? Or even Dare?" The Raven Riders Motorcycle Club's founder; the founder's sister, who'd escaped an abusive marriage and recently survived an attack on the club; and the club's current president all seemed like good choices to Cora. Much better than . . . the person Sam was currently staring at.

He shrugged with one shoulder. "I was hoping . . . you'd let me interview you."

"That's, um, really flattering, Sam. But . . ." Geez, how embarrassing was this to admit? "I'm not all that admirable."

In the positive column, she was a high school graduate, had turned out to be pretty good with kids, loved animals, and could concoct a good runaway plan when necessary. Cora rated herself as a better-than-average friend, and seemed to be able to make people laugh. In the negative, she'd recently been kidnapped by a gang and rescued by a biker club, and now resided with that club while she figured out what the heck to do with her life. And that wasn't even considering what'd happened with her father, back before she'd run . . .

Which she refused to let herself think about just then.

"To me you are," Sam mumbled, suddenly fascinated with the surface of the table.

What the heck was she supposed to say to that? When it was possibly one of the nicest things any human being had ever said to her . . . She eased into a seat. "Really?"

He nodded and finally met her eye. "You're kinda funny," he said.

"Just kinda?" She winked.

Sam's grin was reluctant in that preteen way of his. "I mean, you have your moments."

Cora smirked. "You're really selling my admirable qualities here, Sam Evans."

He shrugged again. "Okay, fine. You're funny. You take good care of us. And you make Ben happy. And I heard you're the one who helped Haven escape from her dad. That was pretty hard core."

"We did it together," Cora said, nearly glowing from the praise. Kids' willingness to just lay their truth out there was one of the things she absolutely loved about being with them. Even if Cora couldn't really agree with Sam's view of her. "That's what friends do for each other." Especially best friends, which Cora and Haven Randall had been since grade school, back before Haven's father had become so possessive that he'd withdrawn her from school to control everyone she saw and everything she did. Cora's father was exactly the opposite—he hadn't cared less what Cora did, where she went, or who she saw—as long as she didn't need his time, attention, or money, which he drank or gambled as fast as he made. She and Haven had sometimes debated which more deserved the *Worst Dad of the Year* trophy. It varied from day to day.

"And you make our house feel . . . alive again," Sam said more quietly. "Like Mom used to."

It was such a stunningly beautiful comment that emotion knotted in Cora's throat. Sam's mom—Slider's wife, Kim—had died young from breast cancer over two years before. The boys rarely mentioned her, and never in Slider's presence. At least, not that Cora had ever witnessed. "Sam," she said around that knot. "That's the sweetest thing anyone has ever said to me."

He blinked up at her, like he wondered if she was teasing him. And she so wasn't. Instead, she was wondering what she could possibly do to actually deserve that kind of compliment. "So, is that a yes?"

Man, she hoped Slider realized how awesome his kids were, because she would give a lot to have children this amazing. Maybe someday that would happen for her. Though, given that people generally preferred to use her rather than keep her, not to mention how much of a mess her life was right now, she was certain that someday was at least a million days off.

"Yeah, that's a yes," she said. "What exactly do you want to know?"

Returning from his only call of the night, Slider parked the tow truck in the lot at Frederick Auto Body and Repair just as the sun turned the morning sky gray. Once, he'd been a master mechanic contemplating owning this place, and now . . . now his life was just like his night had been. A whole lot of nothing punctuated by the occasional unexpected emergency.

He wasn't sure if that was better or worse than the slow, plodding slog of the fourteen months he'd spent knowing catastrophe was coming right at him and his boys, yet unable to do a goddamn thing about it.

But that was cancer for you. Fuck you very much.

Sad truth was, though, that catastrophe had been coming for the Evans men one way or the other, hadn't it?

Damn it all to hell.

Slider punched out. Drove home. Heaved a big breath before he went inside.

God, he hated this house.

Its ghosts, its memories, Kim's touch in every room and on every surface. He couldn't breathe inside this house.

He went in anyway.

Noise. Voices. Laughter.

He found the source of it all in the kitchen.

Sam and Ben sat at the kitchen table with the babysitter, who was demonstrating how to hang a spoon from her nose.

The babysitter.

That was how he thought of her. How he *had* to think of her sometimes. Because if he thought of her as Cora, then he might think of her as a woman. And if he thought of her as a woman, he might take note of the soft waves of her sunny blond hair, or the flare of her hips, or the way the playful glint in her bright green eyes matched the mischievousness of her smile or the sarcasm in her voice.

And Slider couldn't do any of that.

Not when the last time had gone so very wrong—and in ways no one else in his life even knew.

"Dad!" Ben called, shoving up from his seat and sending milk and Cheerios sloshing from his bowl. He rounded the table.

"Little man," Slider said, giving him a squeeze when the boy's body hit him at full speed. "Sleep okay?"

"Yeah," Ben said. "We saved you ice cream."

"Hey, Dad," Sam said, taking his bowl to the sink and cleaning up his brother's mess—without having to be asked. Sometimes Slider had to wonder which of them was the adult around here anymore, and didn't that make him feel like fucking Dad of the Year.

"Ice cream?" he asked, eyeing the babysitter where she stood at the sink rinsing the breakfast dishes.

She threw a tentative smile over her shoulder. "I promised them a party, so I texted Phoenix and asked him to bring over a couple half gallons and all the fixings for a sundae-building party."

"Phoenix taught me how to make a banana split," Ben said, talking a mile a minute. "Except marshmallow goop is gross. And cherries stain the ice cream and make everything red which is even grosser."

Cora chuckled. "I didn't see any ice cream left in your bowl, Bean."

The boy turned a smile on her that was going to break hearts one day. "Well, no . . ."

"Go brush your teeth and put on your shoes," she said, shaking her head with an indulgent smile. "Bus will be here in ten minutes."

Slider watched the series of exchanges like he was merely an observer. Like he was on the outside looking in. And it was an apt description, wasn't it? The babysitter was the one giving his kids a reason to smile and be happy. And his club brother, Phoenix Creed, had apparently had a hand in that, too.

It should've all struck him as completely normal. A happy, functional family. But normal . . . Jesus, normal killed him these days. It really did. He was glad for it, for Ben's and Sam's sakes. But otherwise, normal felt a whole lot like trying to swallow crushed glass. It'd been like that ever since Kim had told him what had been going on with her . . .

Cora's voice forced away the thoughts. "Can I make you something to eat?"

He slanted a glance at her, studiously ignoring the little intimacies of her appearance—like that her makeup-free face and cute pigtails revealed that she'd woken up in his house, like that the oversized sweatshirt she wore over a pair of boxers likely covered the clothes in which she'd slept, like that she'd painted the second toenail on each foot a different color from the rest.

None of which he had any business noticing. "I'm good," he said, the lie obvious to both of them, but what the hell did that really matter? "Thanks," he forced himself to add.

Sam returned first to the kitchen, and Slider was grateful for the interference.

"Finish your homework?" he asked his boy.

"Yeah," Sam said, throwing a shy smile at Cora—who was suddenly blushing a beautiful, brilliant cherry red that made Slider pull a double take. It was on the tip of his tongue to ask, but then the whirlwind that was his six-year-old came into the kitchen, and, after a couple of quick good-byes, Cora was bustling them both out the front door for the bus.

The house resoundingly quiet now, he glanced out the front door. And found Cora walking up the driveway while holding the boys' hands—both of them, even Sam, who hadn't offered or sought a hug in . . . well, just over two years. The kids' laughter just reached him even from this distance, their body language relaxed, happy, and open despite the fact that the gray morning had turned drizzly.

Damn, there was no denying this woman was good with them. Even more, she was good *for* them. Much better than the older neighbor lady had been, with her smoking and bad knees and dislike of noise.

Slider had gotten lucky finding Cora. Once, he might've thought that she'd come along right when they needed her, as if the universe had personally done him a solid by dropping Cora Campbell in the Ravens' lap. But Slider didn't believe in luck or fate or divine providence, and he knew one day, Cora would leave him, too.

Everybody did.

They were just using each other in the meantime.

Been there, done that, got the motherfucking T-shirt.

When Cora returned five minutes later, he stood at the kitchen counter chugging a glass of water.

"So, I'll get changed," she said, thumbing over her shoulder. He gave her a nod and tried not to let his gaze try to connect the rain droplets that darkened her sweatshirt and slicked the exposed skin of her legs. "But I wanted to mention that we need to go grocery shopping."

We. The word was a total sucker punch.

And it made him need to get her the hell out of his house. At least for a few hours. Because the only *we* Slider did now was the kind he'd created with his own blood. "I'll get on it."

She didn't leave to get dressed like he expected her to. Instead, she lingered, then finally said, "I know you're on again tonight and need to sleep. Maybe . . . I could get Bunny to take me and we'll drop everything off here later."

"That's okay," he said, shaking his head.

"Or, if it's easier, I could even hang here today and you could take me when you wake up. God knows I don't have anywhere special I need to be, so it wouldn't be a problem . . ."

He pictured her staying in his house in a sudden flash of images—her making lunch, her cuddled into the corner of the couch watching TV, her stepping out of the bathroom, hair wet from a shower, and the sweet-smelling scent of her lotion trailing after her . . . Twin reactions coursed through him. A yearning for the companionship of another adult sharing his space and his life. And a kneejerk fight-or-flight *hell no* that both left him unsettled and pissed him off.

All of which meant she had to go. Now.

"Jesus, I said I'll take care of it. I don't need you." Something akin to panic had the words coming out more harshly than he'd intended, and his brain was already scrambling to clean up the mess his mouth had made. "To do it, I mean. I don't need you for shopping. Okay? I got it."

"Right. Of course," she said, backing out of the room, green eyes flashing with an emotion he couldn't name.

And he was a giant asshole. He scrubbed his face on a long sigh and waited for her to come back so he could drive her home. And apologize.

He waited. And waited.

What the hell?

"Uh, Cora, you ready?" he called out, making sure his tone lacked the frustration he felt with himself. Two-plus years of withdrawing from the world around him had left him all kinds of rusty at interacting like a normal human being.

When there was no response, he waited a few more minutes. Guilt a weight on his shoulders, Slider finally went back down the hall toward the family room, where she slept on the couch because she'd long ago refused his offer to use his bed on nights when he wasn't home. The downstairs bathroom was empty. And so was the family room. A creeping apprehension squeezed his chest when he noticed that her bag was gone and the blankets she used were back in their neat little stack, too.

No. No, no. Shit.

His gaze lifted to the door to the back porch, and that was when he knew.

She'd left.

He'd been an asshole, and she'd left. And now she was out on the street.

Sonofabitch.

Slider imagined telling Sam and Ben that Cora wasn't coming anymore, that he'd upset her and chased her away, and something close to horror flashed through his gut. He had to fix this. He had to fix it now.

Want More Hot Contemporary Romance from Laura Kaye?

CHECK OUT:

THE RAVEN RIDERS SERIES
**Brotherhood. Club. Family.
They live and ride by their own rules.
These are the Raven Riders...**

RIDE HARD (RAVEN RIDERS #1)

Raven Riders Motorcycle Club President Dare Kenyon rides hard and values loyalty above all else. He'll do anything to protect the brotherhood of bikers—the only family he's got—as well as those who can't defend themselves. So when beautiful but mistrustful Haven Randall lands on the club's doorstep scared that she's being hunted, Dare takes her in, swears to keep her safe, and pushes to learn the secrets overshadowing her pretty smile before it's too late.

RIDE ROUGH (RAVEN RIDERS #2)

Alexa Harmon thought she had it all—the security of a good job, a beautiful home, and a pow-erful, charming fiancé who offered the life she never had growing up. But when her dream quickly turns into a nightmare, Alexa realizes she's fallen for a façade she can't escape—until her ex-boyfriend and Raven Riders MC vice-president Maverick Ryland offers her a way out. Forced to-gether to keep Alexa safe, their powerful attraction reignites and Maverick determines to do what-ever it takes to earn a second chance—one Alexa is tempted to give. But her ex-fiancé isn't going to let her go without a fight, one that will threaten everything they both hold dear.

RIDE WILD (RAVEN RIDERS #3)

Wild with grief over the death of his wife, Sam "Slider" Evans merely lives for his two sons. Nothing holds his interest anymore—not even riding his bike or his membership in the Raven Riders Motorcycle Club. But then he hires Cora Campbell to be his nanny. Cora adores Slider's sweet boys, but never expected the red-hot attraction to their brooding, sexy father. If only he would notice her… Slider does see the beautiful, fun-loving woman he invited into his home. She makes him feel too much, and he both hates it and yearns for it. But when Cora witnesses something she shouldn't have, the new lives they've only just discovered are threatened. Now Slider must claim—and protect—what's his before it's too late.

THE HARD INK SERIES
**Five dishonored soldiers
Former Special Forces
One last mission
These are the men of Hard Ink…**

HARD AS IT GETS (HARD INK #1)

Trouble just walked into Nicholas Rixey's tattoo parlor.

Becca Merritt is warm, sexy, whole-some—pure temptation to a very jaded Nick. He's left his military life behind to become co-owner of Hard Ink Tattoo, but Becca is his ex-commander's daughter. Loyalty won't let him turn her away. Lust has plenty to do with it too. With her brother presumed kidnapped, Becca needs Nick. She just wasn't expecting to want him so much. As their investigation turns into all-out war with an organized crime ring, only Nick can protect her. And only Becca can heal the scars no one else sees.

Hard As You Can (Hard Ink #2)

Shane McCallan doesn't turn his back on a friend in need, especially a former Special Forces teammate running a dangerous, off-the-books operation. Nor can he walk away from Crystal, the gorgeous blonde waitress is hiding secrets she doesn't want him to uncover. Too bad. He's exactly the man she needs to protect her sister, her life, and her heart. All he has to do is convince her that when something feels this good, you hold on as hard as you can—and never let go.

Hard to Hold On To (Hard Ink #2.5)

Edward "Easy" Cantrell knows better than most the pain of not being able to save those he loves—which is why he is not going to let Jenna Dean, the woman he helped rescue from a gang, out of his sight. He may have just met her, but Jenna's the first person to make him feel alive since that devastating day in the desert more than a year ago. As the pair are thrust together while chaos reigns around them, they both know one thing: the things in life most worth having are the hardest to hold on to.

Hard to Come By (Hard Ink #3)

When a sexy stranger asks questions about her brother, Emilie Garza is torn between loyalty to the brother she once idolized and fear of the war-changed man he's become. Derek DiMarzio's easy smile and quiet strength tempt Emilie to open up, igniting the desire between them and leading Derek to crave a woman he shouldn't trust. Now, Derek and Emilie must prove where their loyal-ties lie before hearts are broken and lives are lost. Because love is too hard to come by to let slip away...

Hard to Be Good (Hard Ink #3.5)

Hard Ink Tattoo owner Jeremy Rixey has taken on his brother's stateside fight against the forc-es that nearly killed Nick and his Special Forces team a year before. Now, Jeremy's whole world has been turned upside down—not the least of which by kidnapping victim Charlie Merritt, a bril-liant, quiet blond man who tempts Jeremy to settle down for the first time ever. With tragedy and chaos all around them, temptation flashes hot, and Jeremy and Charlie can't help but wonder why they're trying so hard to be good...

Hard to Let Go (Hard Ink #4)

Beckett Murda hates to dwell on the past. But his investigation into the ambush that killed half his Special Forces team and ended his Army career gives him little choice. Just when his team learns how powerful their enemies are, hard-ass Beckett encounters his biggest complication yet—his friend's younger sister, seductive, feisty Katherine Rixey. When Kat joins the fight, she lands straight in Beckett's sights . . . and in his arms. Not to mention their enemies' crosshairs. Now Beckett and Kat must set aside their differences to work together, because the only thing sweeter than justice is finding love and never letting go.

HARD AS STEEL (HARD INK #4.5)

After identifying her employer's dangerous enemies, Jessica Jakes takes refuge at the compound of the Raven Riders Motorcycle Club. Fellow Hard Ink tattooist and Raven leader Ike Young promises to keep Jess safe for as long as it takes, which would be perfect if his close, personal, round-the-clock protection didn't make it so hard to hide just how much she wants him—and al-ways has. The last thing Ike needs is alone time with the sexiest woman he's ever known, one he's purposely kept at a distance for years. Now, Ike's not sure he can keep his hands or his heart to himself—or that he even wants to anymore.

HARD EVER AFTER (HARD INK #5)

After a long battle to discover the truth, the men and women of Hard Ink have a lot to celebrate, especially the wedding of two of their own—Nick Rixey and Becca Merritt, whose hard-fought love deserves a happy ending. But an old menace they thought long gone reemerges, threatening the peace they've only just found. Now, for one last time, Nick and Becca must fight for their al-ways and forever.

HARD TO SERVE (HARD INK #5.5)

To protect and serve is all Detective Kyler Vance ever wanted to do, so when Internal Affairs investigates him as part of the new police commissioner's bid to oust corruption, everything is on the line. Which makes meeting smart, gorgeous submissive, Mia Breslin, at an exclusive play club the perfect distraction.

Their scorching scenes lure them to play together again and again. But then Kyler runs into Mia at work and learns that he's been dominating the daughter of the hard-ass boss who has it in for him. Now Kyler must choose between life-long duty and forbidden desire before Mia finds another who's not so hard to serve.

THE HEARTS IN DARKNESS DUET

HEARTS IN DARKNESS
(HEARTS IN DARKNESS DUET #1)

Two strangers. Four hours. One pitch-black elevator.

Makenna James thinks her day can't get any worse, until she finds herself stranded in a pitch-black elevator with a complete stranger. Caden Grayson is amused when a harried redhead dashes into his elevator fumbling her bags and cell phone, but his amusement turns to panic when the power fails. Despite his piercings, tats, and vicious scar, he's terrified of the dark and confined spaces. Now, he's trapped in his own worst nightmare. To fight fear, they must reach out and open up. With no preconceived notions based on looks to hold them back, they discover just how much they have in common. In the warming darkness, attraction grows and sparks fly, but will they feel the same when the lights come back on?

LOVE IN THE LIGHT
(HEARTS IN DARKNESS DUET #2)

Two hearts in the darkness...must fight for love in the light...

Makenna James and Caden Grayson have been inseparable

since the day they were trapped in a pitch-black elevator and found acceptance and love in the arms of a stranger. Makenna hopes that night put them on the path to forever—which can't happen until she introduces her tattooed, pierced, and scarred boyfriend to her father and three over-protective brothers. Haunted by a child-hood tragedy and the loss of his family, Caden never thought he'd find the love he shares with Makenna. But the deeper he falls, the more he fears the devastation sure to come if he ever lost her, too. When meeting her family doesn't go smoothly, Caden questions whether Makenna deserves someone better, stronger, and just more…normal. Maybe they're just too different—and he's far too damaged—after all…

THE HEROES SERIES

HER FORBIDDEN HERO (HEROES #1)

Former Army Special Forces Sgt. Marco Vieri has never thought of Alyssa Scott as more than his best friend's little sister, but her return home changes that…and challenges him to keep his war-borne demons at bay. Marco's not the same person he was back when he protected Alyssa from her abusive father, and he's not about to let her see the mess he's become. But Alyssa's not looking for protection—not anymore. Now that she's back in his life, she's determined to heal her forbidden hero one touch at a time…

ONE NIGHT WITH A HERO (HEROES #2)

After growing up with an abusive, alcoholic father, Army Special Forces Sgt. Brady Scott vowed never to marry or have kids. Sent stateside to get his head on straight—and his anger in check—Brady's looking for a distraction. He finds it in Joss

Daniels, his beautiful new neighbor whose one-night-only offer for hot sex leads to more. Suddenly, Brady's not so sure he can stay away. But when Joss discovers she's pregnant, Brady's rejection leaves her feeling abandoned. Now, they must overcome their fears before they lose the love and security they've found in each other, but can they let go of the past to create a future together?

About Laura Kaye

LAURA IS THE NEW YORK Times and USA Today bestselling author of thirty books in contemporary and erotic romance and romantic suspense, including the Blasphemy, Hard Ink, and Raven Riders series. Growing up, Laura's large extended family believed in the supernatural, and family lore involving angels, ghosts, and evil-eye curses cemented in Laura a life-long fascination with storytelling and all things paranormal. Laura also writes historical fiction as the NYT bestselling author, Laura Kamoie. She lives in Maryland with her husband and two daughters, and appreciates her view of the Chesapeake Bay every day.

Learn more at **www.LauraKayeAuthor.com**

Made in the USA
Middletown, DE
19 March 2022